Blaze

Dear Reader,

I'm thrilled to be back with another hot vampire series for Harlequin Blaze! Meet Cody Braddock, the youngest of the notorious Braddock Brothers, a confederate raiding group who plundered Union armies during the Civil War. Cody is now a champion bull rider, just one win shy of setting a PBR record for the most consecutive championships. He's also *this* close to finding the vampire who murdered his family and doomed him to an eternity of darkness. Revenge is the only thing on Cody's mind when he rides into Skull Creek, Texas, and meets Miranda Rivers.

Okay, so maybe it's not the *only* thing.

I hope you enjoy this first book featuring the ultra-sexy Braddock brothers!

I love to hear from readers. You can visit me online at www.kimberlyraye.com or write to me c/o Harlequin Books, 225 Duncan Mill Road, Don Mills, Ontario M3B 3K9, Canada.

Much love from deep in the heart!

Kimberly Raye

Kimberly Raye

CODY

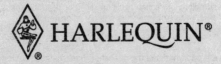

TORONTO • NEW YORK • LONDON
AMSTERDAM • PARIS • SYDNEY • HAMBURG
STOCKHOLM • ATHENS • TOKYO • MILAN • MADRID
PRAGUE • WARSAW • BUDAPEST • AUCKLAND

Recycling programs
for this product may
not exist in your area.

ISBN-13: 978-0-373-79500-0

CODY

Copyright © 2009 by Kimberly Groff.

ABOUT THE AUTHOR

Bestselling author Kimberly Raye started her first novel in high school and has been writing ever since. Currently she is writing a romantic vampire mystery series for Ballantine Books that is in development with ABC for a television pilot. She also writes steamy contemporary reads for the Harlequin Blaze line. Kim lives deep in the heart of the Texas Hill Country with her very own cowboy, Curt, and their young children. She's an avid reader who loves Diet Dr. Pepper, chocolate, Toby Keith, chocolate, alpha males (*especially* vampires) and chocolate. Kim also loves to hear from readers. You can visit her online at www.kimberlyraye.com.

Books by Kimberly Raye

This book is dedicated to my very own cowboy,
Curt.
He's not a bloodsucker, but he's still
the sexiest man I know.
I love you, honey!

Prologue

Texas, 1865

THE ONLY THING ON CODY Braddock's mind as he pushed his horse the last mile toward the Circle B was sliding his cock into a warm, willing woman.

It had been months since he'd touched soft, fragrant skin. Smelled the sweet scent of desire. Heard the deep, throaty moans of pure, exquisite pleasure.

He wanted it. He needed it. Which meant his already overdue homecoming would have to wait that much longer.

"I'll ride in later," he called out to his older brothers, Brent and Travis, who trotted up front. Colton, the oldest, led the group several yards up ahead. He was anxious.

Cody couldn't blame him. If he'd had a woman half as sweet as Rose waiting for him, he'd have been anxious to get home, too. But one woman wasn't his style.

Cody was the youngest. The wildest. And the reason the Braddock Brothers had ridden off four years ago to make a name for themselves as the most indestructible raiding group the Union army had ever had the misfortune to see.

Actually, his three brothers had ridden after him to

talk some sense and haul him back by his bootstraps. They'd made a pact as kids to look out for each other. To stick together. They'd had to. Their father had abandoned them when Cody had been a little over five. Lyle Braddock had left his home, his wife and his four boys to ride off in hot pursuit of some saloon whore.

They hadn't seen him since. Rumor had it Lyle had died in a bar fight, but no one really knew for sure. Nor did they care. They'd been too busy taking care of each other to worry over a man who'd never been much of a father.

When Cody had up and left to join the Confederate cause, his brothers had ridden along to keep an eye on him. They'd seized supplies and helped Confederate troops and given Quantrill and his boys a run for their money when it came to notoriety.

But the war was over now. The South had lost.

Time to go home.

A wave of restlessness swept through him and his chest tightened. He jerked his reins and steered his horse east. He left his brothers behind and headed toward the Red Rooster, the one and only saloon in the territory.

A brunette. That's what he wanted first. Then a redhead. A blonde after that. Hell, maybe he'd splurge and go for all three at once. He had a lot of time to kill now that the Braddock Brothers were officially disbanded.

He picked up his pace, desperate to burn off the sudden rush of anxiety and defeat that clung to him.

He'd done his best, but it hadn't been good enough. *He* hadn't been good enough. Not during the war, and sure as hell not before.

"You're not a kid, Cody. Time to get the ants out of your britches and man up."

His oldest brother's voice followed him, pushing him harder and faster. He was tired of thinking. About the war. About going home. About *being* at home.

He'd never been good in any one spot for too long.

Like father, like son.

The notion drove him harder, faster, because as much as he'd promised his brothers he'd give ranching a nice, solid try again, the thought of being stuck in any one place made him feel like he was choking. He needed a few hours first. Time to burn up the energy bubbling inside him. The restlessness. Then he could do it.

He would.

He owed them. They'd saved his ass too many times to count over the past few years and so he intended to bury his damned wanderlust and pull his weight at the Circle B once and for all.

His father might not have been able to do it, but Cody damn well could—

His brain scrambled to a stop as his nostrils flared with the pungent scent of smoke. Whipping his head around, he spotted the black billows that rose in the far distance.

What the…?

A sense of foreboding slithered around his spine. Goosebumps chased up and down his arms and his gut hollowed out. He almost pitched backward as he hauled the horse around.

Seconds later, he was riding hellbent for leather toward his family's spread. Toward his mother. His sister-in-law. His nephew.

They'd been the ones left at home when the brothers had ridden off four years ago. Just the three of them, a ranch foreman and a half dozen hands. Little match for an attack. Indian or otherwise.

The smoke grew thicker, clawing at his nose and clogging up his lungs. He covered his mouth and pushed harder until he finally broke through the trees and found himself smack dab in the middle of hell.

Flames licked at the main house where he'd grown up. Fire consumed the three surrounding barns. Frightened horses stomped around, dodging the smoke and the flames as they fought for a way out of the chaos. Shouts carried from the barn and fear spiraled through him. Cody jumped off his horse, determined to find his brothers and figure out what the hell was going on.

Something bad.

Something *really* bad.

He started forward, but a faint whimper stalled him in his tracks.

He whirled toward the house and blinked against the burning smoke and heat. Sparks flew and the right corner of the house caved in. He hauled his collar up and over his mouth and pushed through the fog. His eyes burned and watered as he drank in his surroundings. The sound slid into his ears again and drew him toward the left and the familiar pink dress visible just beneath the porch steps.

He was on the woman in a heartbeat, pulling her away from the fast crumbling house.

Sis Braddock's eyes were closed, her face covered with soot. Blood pumped from the deep gash across the side of her neck and soaked her dress. So much blood.

"Ma," Cody breathed and the woman's eyelids flickered open.

"I—I tried to stop him," she gurgled. Her fingers tightened on the iron brand clutched in her grip. Blood caked the familiar B and sucker-punched Cody right in his gut. "But…h-he started…fire." A line of red spurted from the corner of her mouth and pain twisted her features. "I—I couldn't…get to…them."

"Where's Rose and Michael?"

But he already knew. Deep in his gut, he knew even before she croaked out the one word.

"Dead." She shuddered. Her chest jerked as she tried to breathe. The blood gushed faster. "You came back," she managed, the words soft and gurgled. "I knew you would. I knew…"

Because she'd believed in him when no one else had. When he'd been five years old and old Mister Arnold had accused him of stealing a pig. When he'd been twelve and Pastor Willard had blamed him for the missing hymnals.

She'd been wrong on both counts, just as she'd been wrong about his father. She'd always believed Lyle would change his mind and come back. That he would straighten up and come home.

"My boy…" Her body shuddered. The brand slipped from her hands and clattered to the ground.

"I'm here, Ma. I'm *here*." He shook her, but it was too late. Her body was limp. Lifeless. *"No!"*

Anger and denial whirled around Cody, twining around him and squeezing tight until he couldn't breathe. He grabbed the brand and staggered to his feet.

"I tried to stop him."

Her desperate words echoed in his head, driving him around, toward the barn and the chaos and *him.*

It hadn't been Indians. He would have heard the war cries and seen the evidence. This was different.

Evil.

Fire crackled. Wood crumbled. Sparks spewed. Cody didn't care. He headed straight for hell, determined to take whoever was responsible with him.

He made it three steps before the back of his skull exploded with pain and his knees buckled.

He hit the dirt facedown, the brand clutched in his hand. A man's voice slid into his ears.

"You shouldn't have come back. You don't belong here anymore."

But he did.

This was his home.

His family.

His.

And he wasn't letting go of it without a fight.

He clutched the brand tighter and then everything went black.

1

Texas, Present Day

HE HADN'T HAD SEX IN forty-eight hours.

While two days of deprivation was nothing for most men, Cody Braddock wasn't the average guy. He was a hell-raising, adrenaline-loving, nine-time Professional Bull Riders champion—known to the world as Cody "Balls to the Wall" Boyd—just weeks away from record-breaking buckle number ten.

He was also a vampire who fed off of blood and sex.

Cody was desperate for both as he walked into the crowded Sixth Street bar in the heart of Austin, Texas.

A Nickelback song blasted from the loudspeakers and vibrated the walls. A splatter of colored lights bounced off the sea of writhing bodies that filled the small dance floor. The air reeked of beer and stale cigarette smoke.

It was the kind of place people came to drown their troubles and forget. A bad day. A cheating spouse. An arrogant boss. A stack of unpaid bills.

A little liquid courage, a lot of sex, and all would be right with the world. Or so they thought.

He read that much in their gazes, and what he couldn't see when he made direct eye contact, he felt.

Lust and desperation swirled into a nearly irresistible aphrodisiac that filled his nostrils and lured him deeper inside the club. Body heat pushed and pulled at him from every angle. Dozens of heartbeats mingled together in a steady *ba-bom ba-bom* that echoed in his head and throbbed through his body. A strange awareness crawled up his spine and he glanced to the right.

His gaze collided with a pair of deep, unreadable brown eyes and he quickly realized he wasn't the only one looking for a little action tonight.

He didn't know the guy's name or anything about him. He only knew that the young gun wasn't human and that he'd come to feed. A long time ago, Cody would have been surprised at running into another vampire. They'd been few and far between back when Cody had been turned.

But now…

There were more. They existed side-by-side with humans, feeding on them when the need arose and tossing them when they were finished. They were the ultimate predators. Alluring. Persuasive. Powerful. Invincible. *Deadly.* The moral barometer had slipped away right along with the humanity. Forgotten like a bad day.

For most.

But Cody refused to forget.

He still remembered the last beat of his heart. The last draw of breath. The last flutter of life. The memories haunted him, driving him almost as fiercely as the hunger. To find the vampire who'd slaughtered his family that fateful night and destroy him once and for all.

Cody still had several miles to go before he reached his destination—a small town north of San Antonio, Texas. But he was a hell of a lot closer than he'd been when he'd first seen the copy of *Motorcycle Mania* featuring the trio behind Skull Creek Choppers, the fastest growing custom motorcycle manufacturer in the south.

One glance at the picture and he'd been pulled back to the moment when his life had changed forever. When *he'd* changed. In a fiery blaze, he'd lost everything that mattered to him—his mother, his sister-in-law, his nephew, his brothers, his home.

Not that Brent, Travis and Colton were dead like the others. His brothers had suffered a fate far worse than a mortal death—they'd been turned just as Cody had. They lived in isolation now, feeding off blood and sex, doomed to an eternity of hunger. One eaten up by guilt, one driven by anger, one so indifferent he didn't give a shit about anyone or anything.

And Garret Sawyer, the creative genius behind SCC, was the vampire responsible.

Cody could still remember the pain in his skull, the blackness. When he'd regained consciousness, it had been Sawyer who'd loomed over him, his fangs bared, his face and clothes covered in soot and blood. He'd held a knife in his hand.

The same knife he'd used to kill Cody's mother.

Cody's oldest brother Colton had seen Sawyer, as well. The same face. The blood. The knife.

It was Sawyer, all right. It had to be.

And Cody intended to make him pay for what he'd

done. Maybe then the what-ifs would stop once and for all.

What if he hadn't left his brothers to head for town?

What if he'd ridden in a minute sooner?

What if he'd been there?

Cody forced aside the endless questions and concentrated on the task at hand—feeding and gathering his strength.

He shifted his attention back to the younger vampire. He gave a quick nod. The vamp replied in kind before turning back to the woman next to him. He smiled and the brunette practically swooned. A split second later, he steered her toward the rear exit.

Cody's gut tightened and his mouth watered, and anxiety rushed through him. His shoulder cried, reminding him of yesterday's practice ride on an ornery bull named Mabel prior to picking up the *Motorcycle Mania* issue. While vampires weren't susceptible to mortal injuries, they still felt pain. More so than the average human thanks to heightened senses. Translation—when he hurt, he friggin' *hurt*.

Not for long though.

He stared through the dim interior and met a pair of deep blue eyes rimmed in a quarter inch of black eyeliner.

Her name was Laura and this was the first time she and her new boyfriend had gone out on the town as a couple. She loved the guy who stood next to her with his arm around her waist, but she wished he wouldn't act so damned possessive. It wasn't like she was going to ditch him. Although she might consider it if the hot-looking cowboy staring at her gave the slightest indication that he had the same thing in mind.

The arm tightened around her waist and Cody shifted his gaze to her companion. His name was Mark and he worked on a road crew. He didn't like men looking at his woman and he sure as hell didn't like his woman looking at any men.

Cody tipped his hat and shifted his gaze elsewhere. There were too many available women to get himself stuck in a love triangle. Especially when he wasn't looking for love, or anything close. Not that such a thing existed. He'd been around over one hundred and fifty years and never in all that time had he seen anything close to such an emotion. Like? Yes. Lust? Hell, yes. But one man/one woman, to have and to hold, 'til death do us part *love?*

It just didn't exist. Not for a vampire like Cody, or the man he'd once been.

A man just like his father.

He ignored the thought. It didn't matter now. The only thing that mattered to him was sustenance.

Strength.

Sex.

His attention shifted to one of the bar maids loading her tray with longnecks. As if she sensed his attention, her gaze snapped to his and all of her secrets whispered through his head. Her name was Jenna. Her husband neglected her and so she'd started wearing her shorts shorter and her T-shirts tighter. She mainly flirted for bigger tips, but she'd been known to sleep with one or two if the chemistry—or the money—was right.

Ditto for number one.

She smiled and he tipped his hat.

And then he turned away because Cody had a strict *Hell no!* policy when it came to married women. They rated right up there with the innocent, naive types because, inevitably, they wanted more from him than a few hours of bliss.

They wanted a real relationship, and he wasn't in any position to stick around and deliver. His survival depended on knowing when to cut and run. Sure, he was riding a high with his rodeo career right now, but the end was fast approaching. Especially with Benny James hot on his tail.

James was a reporter for *No Bull,* a fanzine type magazine about the rodeo circuit. He'd put in through Cody's publicist for an interview several months ago, which Cody had declined. The reporter hadn't taken the news too kindly and he'd made it his mission in life to get the dirt on PBR's hottest star. He'd starting mentioning Cody in his monthly *Who's Who* column, calling him the Lone Ranger and stirring as much speculation as possible. About Cody's extremely private lifestyle. His uncanny athletic prowess. His high tolerance for pain.

Bull riding was a tough profession and there wasn't a rider out there who didn't wear the battle scars. Broken bones. Bruises. But not Cody. The only scar he had came from a case knife back during a particularly nasty raid on a Union general who'd been holding Confederate prisoners. He'd been a man then and vulnerable.

He was the ultimate riding machine now. Strong. Fearless. Invincible. Crazy.

Then again, he'd always been a little crazy. Impulsive. Wild. Not a good thing for a vampire desperate to keep a low profile.

James was onto him. While the man might not have figured out Cody's true identity or his bloodsucking secret, he knew something was up.

And now, thanks to the column, so did everyone else.

The entire rodeo world was questioning how long the infamous Cody Boyd could keep going at such a brutal pace. It was just a matter of time before a vampire slayer picked up on the speculation and put the puzzle pieces together.

Cody had been trying his best to keep his impulses in check, but the effort had made little difference. He needed to quit the circuit completely. Go back to being just plain old Cody Braddock and working the horse ranches the way he'd done for the past one hundred years. He would, just as soon as *Balls to the Wall* Boyd broke the PBR record for the most consecutive championships. One more season, and it was his.

Until then…

His gaze shifted to the blonde standing near the corner of the L-shaped bar.

She had *fast and fleeting* written all over her. From the skimpy pink dress that outlined a pair of porn star breasts, to the hot pink cowboy boots that made her legs seem long and endless. Full, thick platinum hair framed her heart-shaped face and plunged past her shoulders.

She had bright sparkling eyes as potent as a bottle of Jack Daniels fringed with thick black lashes. An extra layer of pink lipstick accented her lush mouth and stirred an image so evocative that his cock gave a quick salute.

A reaction that tightened every muscle in his body and set off his internal alarm.

A definite first because he'd never been the least bit interested in a woman's mouth, no matter how attractive, or how experienced. Not when he'd been a man—young and wild and as horny as the day was long—and not now.

He didn't waste his time with soft kisses or gentle touches. He took the lead in bed, stirring and provoking until his partner exploded and he drank in the vibrant energy of her climax.

Not that he didn't try to get his O on every now and then, too. What red-blooded male—man or vampire— *didn't* want to come? But Cody always found himself getting caught up in the woman's big moment rather than his own, and once the beast was fed, he lost his enthusiasm. Which explained why he hadn't had an actual orgasm with a woman since he'd opened his eyes as a vampire.

He enjoyed himself. He fed. But he never came.

He had no doubt now would be any different. Even if the lust burning up his veins felt hotter than it usually did. More potent.

His gut clenched and his dick ached. It was all he could do not to cross the room, bend her over the bar, pull up her dress and sink into her hot, lush body.

She looked more than appropriate for what he had

in mind. But while her body said *do me,* her eyes told an altogether different story.

Her name was Miranda Rivers and she was way out of her element. She'd never worn her hot pink cowboy boots. Never been to a bar. Never picked up a stranger. She'd never even drank more than one margarita.

Until tonight.

She was working on her third and she wanted a man. And sex. She wanted to live out just one of her fantasies before she turned her back on all of them and continued down the straight and narrow path she'd been traveling her entire life.

This was her detour.

Her one chance to let her guard down and live out one of her many fantasies.

Perfect, right?

Wrong. While she had a body made for sex, she'd never had an actual orgasm with a man. That's what tonight was all about. Since she hadn't exploded with the few safe, boring men in her past, she'd decided to go for forbidden and exciting.

Problem solved.

Unless the problem wasn't the men.

She was the common denominator. The one constant in each lukewarm encounter. What if she simply wasn't capable of an orgasm?

Her gaze collided with his and he saw the instant spark of lust. A surprising reaction because he hadn't sent any seductive thoughts her way. He hadn't enticed or mesmerized, or anything. She was attracted to him of her own accord.

Heat rolled through his body like a swig of whiskey and sucker punched him right in the gut.

He stiffened. While she might be attracted to him, the last thing he needed was to waste his time on a *what if*. He needed to turn around and walk the other way no matter how lush her body or how full her mouth or how desperate he was to taste her.

He needed a sure thing.

He started to turn away. But then she smiled and his hunger stirred, and he couldn't help himself.

Cody Braddock had been a slave to his impulses far too long to stop now.

2

HE WAS THE SEXIEST COWBOY she'd ever seen.

Which said a lot because Miranda Rivers had become quite the expert over the years.

Thanks entirely to her mother—part-time *B is for Beautiful* independent makeup consultant and full-time buckle bunny—Miranda had witnessed hundreds of Stetsons bobbing through the front door of the single wide trailer where she'd grown up. A parade that had continued as her two older sisters had matured and carried on their mother's weakness for men with tight Wranglers, starched shirts and a wild and reckless charm.

It was a weakness that had eventually killed Chastity Rivers.

She'd fallen too hard, too fast, for a man who'd rejected her. She'd been so devastated that she'd killed herself and left her daughters to finish raising themselves.

Miranda had been fourteen at the time.

Lucy and Robin had been older, sixteen and nineteen, but it had been Miranda who'd stepped up to take the lead in the family. She'd cleaned the house and cooked dinner while her sisters had strutted their stuff, stayed out all night and stirred up as much gossip as possible.

Time had changed little. Lucy worked at a nearby bar and partied away her earnings while Robin played groupie to a local country band.

They were still the baddest girls in town.

They always had been, and Miranda had been guilty by association.

The entire school had started calling her Restroom Randy back during her sophomore year. A nickname she'd been given when Ray McGuire—junior calf roper and the first cowboy to ever catch her eye—had started a running list on the boy's bathroom wall of all the places Miranda Rivers had gotten down and dirty.

Restroom Randy's Hottest Sex Spots.

All lies, of course. He'd been pissed because she'd turned him down in the backseat of his Daddy's Chevy and he'd wanted to get back at her. He'd started the list, claiming they'd gone all the way not only in the Chevy, but in the front loader of his John Deere, the back alley behind the Piggly Wiggly, the gazebo in the middle of town square, the men's restroom at the local drive-in, beneath the bleachers at the football stadium, smack dab in the middle of the local rodeo arena and the front porch of his family's home.

Miranda had seen the list only once. She'd been sixteen and desperate to know why the entire school was snickering behind her back. A quick duck into the boy's john and she'd found out. The various locations written in red marker had branded themselves into her brain. She'd been mortified and determined to lose the Restroom Randy image.

She'd hated being one of *those* girls. Trashy. No

good. An outsider. She'd wanted to fit in. To feel accepted. To feel safe.

She'd never had any security growing up. Nothing that she could count on. Sometimes she'd had lunch at school. Sometimes she hadn't. Sometimes her mother had been home at night. Sometimes she hadn't. Sometimes she'd had her sisters to keep her company. Sometimes they'd been too busy to care. It had been a roller-coaster ride, and Miranda had wanted off.

She'd wanted a smooth, calm carousel tour and so she'd spent her time studying rather than socializing, determined to trade her unstable existence for something solid. She'd graduated at the top of her class and worked her way through college to earn a sociology degree.

She'd been the activities coordinator at the Skull Creek Senior Center for eight years now. A volunteer at the local library for six. She baked cookies for the ladies auxiliary once a month and chaired an annual fundraising committee for the local food bank. She did her best to steer clear of her sisters and surround herself with people she could count on—the old folks at the senior center and the few people around town who didn't hold her past against her. Since Robin spent most of her time on the road and Lucy only showed up when she wanted money, keeping her distance was relatively easy. Even more, Miranda only dated the kind of men that a woman could count on—nice, conservative, professional types who didn't know the first thing about roping a cow or riding a horse or getting down and dirty in a hayloft.

She'd finally found stability, but she was still missing one thing.

Acceptance.

It was close. Her boyfriend of three months had finally proposed to her via e-mail before he'd left yesterday for a seminar in Houston.

It hadn't been the most exciting proposal, but then Greg wasn't the most exciting guy. He wore khakis and white button-down shirts and, as owner of a local dry cleaning chain, spent his days neck-deep in spot cleaner and starch. He was practical. Nice. *Safe.*

He was also well-respected. His father had been the mayor once-upon-a-time and Greg himself served as president of the local chamber of commerce.

When Greg walked into the Piggly Wiggly, the female clerks didn't stare daggers at him and the stock boys didn't leer. When he waved at old Mr. Witherspoon, the man actually nodded instead of spitting a stream of tobacco juice at his shoe.

Miranda wanted the same acceptance. Or, at the very least, civility. Marrying Greg would give her that.

So why haven't you given him an answer yet?

Because. It was a big step. One she didn't feel comfortable taking via the Internet. She wanted to tell him in person. She *would* tell him. He was a good man from a good family and she was definitely marrying him. Even if he wasn't that great in bed.

Sex wasn't everything.

She *knew* that.

At the same time, she couldn't help but wonder what it would be like to have an orgasm with an actual man rather than a battery-operated body part.

Buck was the heavy-duty vibrator she'd purchased

for her twenty-first birthday. Instead of hitting the local honky tonk to celebrate—Lucy's idea—she'd opted to stay home with a frozen pizza and a *Bonanza* marathon. A few episodes featuring Little Joe and she'd had her first case of horny.

Not that she'd inherited her mother's crippling weakness for cowboys.

There was a big difference between an addiction and mild infatuation. Infatuation brought on by an extreme case of denial. She'd developed a *No Cowboy* policy early on and so it only made sense that she'd started fantasizing about the one thing she could never have. A tall, dark man in a Stetson. Touching her. Kissing her. Giving her a delicious, toe-curling orgasm. She'd wondered every now and then what it would feel like, a curiosity that had killed any and all chances of having a bonafide O with any of the men she'd dated. Three to be exact, including Greg.

They hadn't been wild enough, or exciting enough, or cowboy enough.

No big deal. Miranda had wanted more than an orgasm. She'd wanted respect, and so she'd settled for Buck and her *Bonanza* DVDs.

Until last night.

The proposal had served as a wake-up call. A reminder that time was precious and it was slipping away fast. In two weeks, she would accept Greg's offer and then they were getting *married*.

From this day forward.

'Til death do us part.

It was now or never.

Which was why she'd abandoned her party planning for the annual Sock-Hop scheduled next week at the Senior Center, to pull out her hot pink boots—a high school graduation present from her oldest sister Robin—and make the long drive to Austin. For this one night, she was going to lose her inhibitions and *be* Restroom Randy.

Cowboy up!

Her gaze zeroed in on the jeans-clad legs striding toward her. Her attention took a slow walk up, over muscular thighs and an impressive crotch, a trim waist and solid torso, broad shoulders and a corded neck, to his face.

Several days' growth of stubble shadowed his jaw and circled his sensuous mouth. A thin scar zig-zagged its way across one cheek, but it didn't detract from his looks. If anything, it made him seem more rugged and sexy. Dark hair framed his face and brushed the collar of his shirt. Striking silver eyes fringed in thick black lashes peered at her from beneath the brim of his Stetson.

There was nothing respectable about the molten gleam in his gaze. Heat radiated off his body, pushing and pulling at her, luring her closer when every warning bell in her body clamored for her to turn and run. His lips crooked in the faintest grin that said he knew all of her secrets and he wanted her in spite of them.

Because of them.

Her nipples tightened and her legs quivered and she felt the wetness between her thighs.

He stopped a few inches away. His gaze stripped her bare and a ripple of awareness went up her spine. She'd felt naked back at home when she'd slipped on the skimpy clothes, but it was nothing compared to what she felt now.

Naked. Vulnerable. *Hungry.*

The last thought struck and a bolt of heat sizzled through her. The chemistry was more potent than anything she'd ever felt, but there was something more, as well. A strange connection that said the attraction went much deeper than the physical.

She stiffened against the ridiculous notion and ignored the endless questions swimming in her head.

What's your name?

What do you do?

Where are you from?

Are you the real deal?

He was. He wore an air of danger and wildness as comfortably as he wore his form-fitting jeans.

"You can always tell by the boots," her mother had said time and time again.

Her gaze dropped to the worn toes of a pair of black snakeskin Ropers. Scuffed. Dusty. Lived in. An electrical pulse vibrated along her nerve endings.

"I won them at the Houston Livestock Show and Rodeo."

Her gaze swiveled back up and collided with his. "Excuse me?"

"The boots. I took first place last year in Houston. They were part of the prize. The name's Cody Braddock. I'm a bull rider."

He was a bona fide cowboy, all right.

The last man she would *ever* take to the Senior Sock

Hop. Or the weekly church picnic. Or the Veterans of Foreign Wars Bunko night. Or the Chamber of Commerce Christmas party. Or anything in the tiny town of Skull Creek where she'd spent the past ten years trying to outrun her Restroom Randy reputation.

Which made him the perfect man to take to bed right now.

"Why don't we get out of here?" she blurted before she did something really stupid. Like ask him which bull he'd been riding and how long he'd been risking his neck and where he'd been all her life.

One orgasm, she reminded herself. Then the damned curiosity that kept her tossing and turning and fantasizing at night—every night—would be satisfied. She would say yes to Greg and abandon her legacy for good.

"That is, if you're not married," she added. "You aren't married, are you?"

"No."

"You're sure?"

His grin was slow and wicked and her heart stopped for the next few beats. "That's not something that a man forgets, is it?"

"That depends on the man."

His grin faded. "I'm not the marrying kind. Never have been, never will be."

"How about the one-night-stand kind?"

"Is that what you're after?"

"Actually, an hour or so should do it."

His gaze seemed to liquefy, like silver melting and heating. "You don't want me to buy you a drink first?"

"I'm not much of a drinker." Her gaze caught and

held his and she ignored the sizzle of apprehension that went through her. The small voice that whispered she was about to make a huge, huge mistake because one taste wouldn't come close to satisfying her craving and killing her curiosity.

Instead, she focused on the heat simmering in her belly and the tightening between her legs. "So what about it? You interested in a little exercise?"

His mouth drew into a thin line and his brow furrowed, and she had the distinct impression that he was going to turn her down even though he'd been the one to approach her.

Disappointment rushed through her, followed by a burst of anxiety that fed her impatience. She hadn't driven the two hours from Skull Creek to make sure she didn't run into someone from home just to turn around and head back minus a real climax. She was on a mission. Now or never, a voice whispered.

Now.

Please.

The plea echoed through her head, but she managed to keep it to herself. She'd seen her mother beg and plead too many times the morning after, and every time, Mr. Cowboy had always walked away.

She wouldn't subject herself to the same humiliation. If this particular cowboy didn't want her, so be it. No *way* was she getting hung up on any one man. She would simply move on to the next one in line.

Maybe the guy sitting at the far end of the bar.

She'd scoped him out earlier when she'd first arrived, but she hadn't had a chance to talk to him. With polished gray boots, he looked more drugstore than the real deal. But at least he wore a Stetson, his jeans and shirt starched within an inch of their life. While he wasn't her first choice, he would do—

"Let's go." Cody's deep, husky voice shattered her thoughts and drew her attention. Her gaze collided with his and she had the distinct impression he knew exactly what she'd been thinking.

And that he didn't like it one little bit.

Before she could dwell on the crazy notion, his large hand cupped her elbow and steered her around. He had the oddest touch. His fingers weren't hot like most men. But they weren't clammy either. They felt…strong. Purposeful. Determined.

A zing of excitement spiraled through her. Her nipples throbbed. Her thighs shivered.

And then they headed for the nearest exit and what was sure to be the hottest, wildest, most dangerous experience of Miranda's life.

3

YEARS OF BULL RIDING had finally shaken some screws loose.

That was the only explanation for the fact that Cody had just accepted Miranda's offer *and* told her his real name.

"*The name's Cody Braddock.*"

Sweet Jesus. Was he completely *nuts?*

Hungry, he reminded himself. He was starved and so he wasn't thinking straight. That explained why he was now leading Miranda outside, through the back parking lot toward his truck when his common sense screamed otherwise.

That, and he'd always been impulsive. A loose cannon. A wild card. That's what made him so good on the back of a bull. He didn't waste his time thinking. He simply acted.

No way did his sudden change of heart have anything to do with the fact that he wanted to keep her from propositioning any other man. Particularly the asshole at the end of the bar. The guy had a wife at home that he liked to use for a punching bag.

Not that Cody gave a rat's ass if Miranda got mixed

up with a character like that. Hell, he didn't know her from Eve.

It was the hunger, all right.

It clouded his judgment as darkly as it shaded his past.

He tried to tune into the sounds around him. The music drifting from the row of clubs along Sixth Street. The footsteps up and down the nearby sidewalk. The whir of passing traffic and occasional bleep of a horn. But he found himself picking up only her. The steady beat of her heart and the faint in and out of her breaths and the excited flutter of her pulse.

"Stop." Her soft voice pushed inside his head and he turned just as she dug her heels into the asphalt and pulled him to a stop.

"I thought you wanted to get out of here." His gaze collided with hers and he read the doubt that rolled through her. Half of her wanted to turn and run. Before she did something she would surely regret.

At the same time, that's what this moment was all about. Doing something completely and totally opposite of what she usually did. A few moments of fierce and naughty and memorable to see her through the years and years of nothing special that she knew waited in the future.

"Out of *there*." Determination fired her gaze as she glanced around the parking lot. "Here is just fine." And then she leaned up on her tip-toes and pressed her lips to his.

The sudden connection sent a jolt through him. His muscles stiffened and his groin throbbed and he quickly took the lead.

His hands slid around her waist and he pulled her flush against him. He plunged his fingers into her hair and tilted her head back to give himself better access.

She tasted like the sweetest wine and the most decadent sin and he couldn't get enough. He wanted to be inside of her, his cock deep between her legs, his mouth locked on hers.

He wanted it so badly that he nearly pushed her up against a nearby car, shoved her skirt up to her waist and took her right then and there. But she had something else cooked up in her fantasies—a small alley near the rear Exit door—and Cody was all about pleasing his partner.

Especially this one.

Before he could dwell on the outrageous thought, she rubbed her pelvis against his crotch and electricity zapped the head of his penis. The sensation sizzled through him and gripped every nerve ending until his entire body buzzed.

In the blink of an eye, he picked her up and headed for the narrow alley that ran between the club and a neighboring building.

Her eyes went suddenly wide a heartbeat later when she realized they were standing between the two buildings. "How did you move so fast—" she started, but he silenced her with his mouth.

His lips plundered hers, his tongue pushing deep to stroke and explore and leave her breathless. He pressed her up against the brick so that she could feel the pulse of the music from inside. The excitement. And then he leaned into her, his body flush against hers, so that she could feel *his* excitement.

Emotion rolled through her, a mix of wonder and fear and *hurry the hell up*.

"Anyone could walk by," he murmured, feeding her impatience and the dangerous thrill of being caught.

That's why she had no intention of following him back to his hotel room or taking him home with her. She wanted to live on the edge a little while before she plunged over. She needed it. She'd denied herself for so long and now she wanted to experience the forbidden just once.

The information glittered hot and bright in her gaze as she stared back at him for those next few seconds.

She was through relying on her imagination. She wanted to live up to her reputation. Right here. Right now. Despite the fact that she was hours from home with a man she didn't know.

Because of it.

She didn't want any strings any more than he did.

The truth bothered him a hell of a lot more than it should have and Cody stiffened.

He ignored the strange tightening in his chest and focused on the only thing that mattered—pleasuring her. It was her pleasure—her climax—that would feed the beast inside of him.

He caught the neckline of her skimpy top and pushed it down to her waist. Her luscious breasts spilled free. Dipping his head, he caught one rosy nipple between his teeth. He flicked the tip with his tongue before opening his mouth wider. He drew her in and sucked until a moan vibrated up her throat. The sound fed the lust roaring in his veins.

He knew even before he caught the hem of her skirt and felt the bare skin beneath that she wasn't wearing any panties. Pressing one hard thigh between her legs, he forced her wider until she rode him. Her sweet heat rasped against his starched denim.

She gasped and a shudder ripped through her. He leaned back to see her trembling lips and her quivering breasts.

Shock and surprise swam in her smoky gaze. She'd had sex before, but nothing had ever felt like this. So intense and thrilling and *ahhhhh*…

Her pulse beat frantically at the base of her throat, teasing and taunting him. A slow hiss slid past his lips.

He shifted, moving and rubbing, working her until he felt her dampness through the rough fabric of his jeans. The scent of her arousal teased his nostrils and drenched his senses.

He caught her lips in a fierce kiss and plunged his hand between her legs. She was warm and wet and swollen. At the first touch of his fingers, she went ram-rod stiff. A small cry ripped past her lips and just like that, she came apart in his arms.

A sizzling heat pulsed through her body and entered him at every point of contact—his hand between her legs, his mouth on hers, his thigh pressed intimately between hers. He drank in the sweet energy, relished the dizzying rush of life.

But it wasn't enough because he wasn't hilt deep inside of her.

Yet.

He drank in the picture she made, her head thrown

back against the building, her eyes closed, her lips parted and trembling. She grasped at his shoulders as the convulsions ripped through her, feeding him yet making him all the more hungry at the same time.

His vision clouded, going from Technicolor to a bright, vivid purple that washed everything. The pale color of her hair and the smooth column of her throat. Her translucent breasts. The clothes riding her waist.

He fought the growl vibrating up his throat and the sharp graze of his teeth against his tongue. If he bit her, there would be no turning his back or leaving her behind. The connection would be forged.

Strong.

Resilient.

Unbreakable.

"More," she gasped, her eyelids fluttering open.

Before she could focus and see the beast that he knew gleamed in his eyes, he whirled her around and urged her hands flat against the brick.

Her sweet, round ass pushed back against him and he flicked open the button on his jeans. The zipper wasn't nearly as cooperative. Metal strained and popped and the teeth broke. The denim sagged on his hips and he shoved his underwear down so fast that the material ripped. His erection sprang forward, hard and greedy. The ripe head of his cock pressed the slick folds between her legs and she shuddered.

"Wait," Miranda managed, the feel of him poised and ready like a lightning bolt to her sanity. She drew a deep breath to steady her rapid heartbeat and remember that while she'd made up her mind to let go of her inhibitions and satisfy her curiosity, she wasn't kissing caution goodbye.

Her mother had made that mistake.

Three times to be exact.

"We need a condom," she breathed. "I—I brought some with me." She motioned to her purse which lay on the ground near her feet. "In there."

"I've got my own, sugar."

Of course he did. This might be her first time doing something like this, but it obviously wasn't his.

The realization stirred a strange sense of regret. One that quickly drowned in a wave of heat as he retrieved a small packet, ripped it open and worked the latex down his engorged length. She felt the brush of knuckles against her backside as he positioned himself. His thick head nudged apart her slick folds and pressed into her.

She closed her eyes and relished the feel of him pushing inside, stretching and filling her inch by decadent inch.

Slowly.

Slowly.

There.

He stopped, buried completely for a long moment, the pressure so sharp and sweet that her breath caught. Her heart paused. He throbbed and her body contracted. A wave of impatience went through her, making her nipples ache and her legs tremble.

She moved then, arching her back and sucking him deeper, begging for more of the ecstasy she'd tasted only moments before. She was almost there. So close that she could feel the heat licking at her skin.

The hard brick vibrated against her fingertips, a reminder that she wasn't just out of her comfort zone when it came to men, but she was far, far away from the safety of her bedroom. The notion fed her anticipation as much as the sounds drifting from inside the club. The music and the laughter and the voices...

A woman's voice. Clear. Distinct. Close.

"I thought you wanted to go to my place?"

Miranda felt Cody's muscles tense. Her eyes popped open and her head snapped up in time to see the couple that stumbled around the corner of the building a good twenty feet away.

"Screw that," the man murmured. "Let's just do it right here in the alley." He pressed the woman up against the brick. A trash can flanked them and blocked Miranda's view.

But she could still hear them, which meant they could still hear her. And all they had to do was glance up.

Uh-oh.

4

MIRANDA TRIED TO REACH for her tank top which rode her waist, but Cody's hands covered hers, flattening them against the wall as he pressed his body against hers. "Don't move," he breathed.

"Are you kidding me?" she whispered. "What if they see us?"

"What if they do?" His lips grazed her ear as the other couple groped each other. Their laughter drifted above the muted thud of the popular Katy Perry song blasting inside the club. "Would it be so bad to have an audience?"

Yes. That's what she wanted to say. She'd spent far too many years doing the right thing and saying the right thing to stop now. She didn't do things like this. No back alleys. No audience.

At the same time, that was the point entirely.

She didn't do things like *this,* with a man like this, which was why she'd never had an orgasm during the actual act.

That was all about to change.

"Don't think about them," he murmured. "Close your eyes and think about me." He pressed a soft kiss to her temple and added, "About my cock thick and hot inside of you."

One hand slid up her abdomen to her breast and he caught her nipple, and she did just that.

She closed her eyes and her senses zeroed in on him. The way he pinched the ripe tip of her nipple and played her until need sizzled up and down her spine. A gasp parted her lips.

"You'd better watch it or they'll hear you. Then they'll notice us for sure." He slid his left arm around her, his fingers skimming her rib cage as he caught her other nipple. Now both hands plucked and rolled the sensitive tips until her knees went weak.

He squeezed at the same moment that he thrust into her and a cry curled up her throat. She caught it before it slipped past her lips and clamped her mouth shut as he started to move.

In and out. Back and forth.

She quickly forgot all about the couple, their voices fading in the clamor of her own desire.

She arched against Cody, drawing him deeper, holding him longer when he tried to pull away.

The pressure between her legs stretched tighter and then *popppppp!* Sensation drenched her and she exploded around him. Her head fell back into the curve of his neck, her lips parted and she couldn't help herself then. She cried out.

He caught the sound with his mouth as he moved faster, plunging harder, deeper, stronger. Convulsions gripped her. She milked him, her slick folds clenching around his throbbing penis until a growl sizzled across her nerve endings.

Wait a second. A *growl?*

The realization pushed through the lusty fog and zapped her back to the present. The cool brick wall and the muted music. Her ears perked, but she heard only the sound of her own breathing.

Duh.

She'd obviously deprived herself for so long that when she'd finally gone for the gusto—that is, a forbidden cowboy—the rush of sensation had been like a cattle prod to an electrical box. Her brain was fried.

He buried himself one last time and leaned into her. His body flattened hers against the brick wall. The rough slab rasped her overly sensitive nipples and desire speared her again. Every nerve in her body sizzled. She closed her eyes, relishing the aftershocks of her release which swept through her and filled up the emptiness inside.

Thank you.

The words whispered through her head and she caught them just before they spilled past her lips. The last thing she wanted was for him to think that she'd been desperate.

Why not?

Desperate was good. Desperate meant she wasn't half as experienced as her mother and sisters. Desperate meant that Miranda Rivers was every bit the good girl she'd been pretending to be over the years.

Not that she'd ever had a doubt. She was nothing like her mother or her sisters. She wasn't a slave to her lust and she certainly didn't share their addiction to cowboys.

This was a one-time thing only.

She ignored the regret that whispered through her,

clamped her eyes shut and simply enjoyed the sensation still rippling through her body.

"Thank *you*," he murmured against her ear after a long, heart-pounding moment, his words echoing her thoughts.

He pulled away and the sudden breeze against her bare skin sent a shiver through her. Or maybe it was the fact that he'd practically read her mind.

"They're gone." His voice whispered through her head, distracting her from the crazy notion.

"That's a—" *relief* died on her lips as she turned to find the alley empty.

Really empty. Not only had the groping couple disappeared, but her tall, dark and luscious cowboy had already cut and run, too.

And she hadn't heard a thing.

No rustle of denim as he'd fastened his pants. No slap of boots against the pavement. No lame excuse to get away without asking for her phone number.

Nothing. As if he'd vanished into thin air.

Or back into the building.

The rear exit was the closest doorway. Chances were he'd made a hasty retreat back inside for another drink. Another woman.

So?

It wasn't as if she expected anything more from him than the past few moments.

He was a cowboy, for heaven's sake. Definitely the *last* man she'd pin her expectations on.

This wasn't about him. It was about her. Her moment of indulgence. A chance to stop fantasizing and experience the real thing with a real man before she pledged herself to the right man.

She drew a breath, ignored the disappointment that whispered through her and gathered up her purse. It was over. Done with. Mission accomplished. Time to go home, forget her stupid fantasies and get on with her life.

She blinked against the sudden tears that burned the backs of her eyes as she headed for the back parking lot and her car.

HE'D ERUPTED LIKE A fucking volcano.

The truth followed Cody as he inched past a couple feeling each other up in the back hallway of the club and pushed through the doorway leading to the men's room.

His nostrils flared and his gut ached. The scent of warm cherries and sweet sex clung to him. His dick still throbbed and the craziest sense of satisfaction bubbled through him.

An orgasm. He'd had an actual *orgasm.*

He flipped on the faucet and shoved his hands beneath the cold water. A few punches of the soap dispenser and he lathered up, desperate to erase the scent, the feel.

Her.

Because he didn't want *her.* She could be any woman. Every woman.

So why had he come this time and not the countless times before?

The question struck and he scrubbed harder. Deprivation, he reminded himself. Forty-eight sexless hours. That was enough to make any vampire a little wacky. He hit the dispenser again and lathered up some more. The less she lingered on his skin, the easier it would be to forget. Her gasp of surprise. Her heartfelt gratitude. Her delicious body which had fit him so perfectly, as if she'd been made for him and only him. His unexpected release.

It had been a helluva long time since he'd reacted that way with any woman.

Try never.

At least not since he'd turned vampire.

The truth weighed down on him as he rinsed his hands. It was a fluke. The right time. Right place.

The right woman.

He ignored the last thought and ducked his head to splash some of the cool liquid onto his face. He caught his dripping reflection in the mirror. Bright purple rimmed the edges of his pupils. His hands tightened on the sink and the color shimmered hotter, brighter.

As satisfied as he felt, he was still hungry. He needed another woman. Now.

Raking a hand through his hair, he grabbed a paper towel, wiped his hands and then headed back out to the bar.

Maybe then he could get the sound of her breathing out of his head. The disappointment that followed her to the car. The fear—

His thoughts careened to a halt as a surge of emotion went through him. In a split second, he saw Miranda standing in the back parking lot. He smelled her terror and felt her surprise as her eyes fixed on the scene unfolding near her.

And for the first time since he'd opened his eyes as a vampire, Cody Braddock was scared shitless.

"PLEASE," CAME THE CHOKED gurgle.

Miranda's gaze pushed through the darkness to the two shadows wedged between a pair of parked cars. Shock and disbelief whirled through her. A reaction that had nothing to do with the woman who sprawled on the ground, blood gushing from her throat, and everything to do with the man leaning over her, lapping at the crimson heat.

The man's head lifted and his furious red gaze collided with Miranda's. His lips pulled back. Blood drip-dropped from a pair of lethal looking fangs. A growl bubbled past his lips and sizzled through the air.

Miranda blinked, but he was still there.

Still a...

No.

Denial rushed through her, followed by a quick burst of raw terror. While there had to be an explanation— no way was this guy a real bloodsucker—he was still dangerous. Murderous.

He took a step toward her and she stumbled away from him. She turned and urged her feet to move.

In a heartbeat, he caught her by the hair and yanked her backward. Her legs went out from under her and she landed flat on her back between the two cars. Her head slammed against the pavement. Pain exploded in her skull and blurred her vision. Not enough, however, to obliterate the man's vicious red glare as he loomed over her.

"Well, lookee here. A two-for-one special." He smiled, revealing his blood-stained teeth which matched the crimson of his eyes. "I'll definitely be shopping here again."

A nightmare. The thought struck and she grasped at it, holding tight. None of this was real. Not the choked gurgles of the woman nearby. Or the vicious vampire leaning over her.

None of it.

But then he hissed, his fangs grew sharper and longer, and Miranda braced herself for a very real death.

5

CODY REACHED THE YOUNG MALE vamp just as he was about to sink his fangs into Miranda's neck.

"She's mine," he growled. He caught the vampire's shoulder and the man's head snapped up. Blood trickled from the prick points on Miranda's neck, but it didn't gush. The vampire hadn't bit deep enough to hit the artery and claim her as his own.

Yet.

The notion bothered him a helluva lot more than it should have considering he wasn't the least bit interested in keeping Miranda for himself. Even if she had been one of the best lays he'd had in a long, *long* time.

Cody shifted his attention to the woman sprawled on the pavement nearby. Her chest rose and fell and tears streamed down her cheeks. The bite marks at her neck pumped blood out onto the pavement. She wasn't dead. Yet. "Haven't you had enough?" he asked the young vampire.

A smile twisted his lips. "There's no such thing."

Damn straight. Cody had just had incredible sex, yet his insides still tightened and clenched. His nostrils flared with the decadent scent of blood. His dick throbbed with the memory of Miranda surrounding him, making him come.

He braced himself and eyed the younger vampire who held her in front of him like a shield. "How old are you?"

"Twenty-four."

"Not your age. How long have you been a vampire?"

The red glint in his eyes cooled just a little and impatience flashed. "Eight months. What does that have to do with anything?"

"The fact that you don't know shows just how disadvantaged you are right now. I've got years on you and a century more experience." His gaze dropped to Miranda. Her eyes were wide open, pure fear swimming in their depths. The urge to protect her surged through him and shook him to the core. "You've had your fun tonight. Back off."

"Or else?"

"Do you really have to ask?" Cody flashed his own fangs and the vampire hissed.

Shit.

The last thing he wanted was to get into a pissing contest with a wet-behind-the-ears fledgling. They could be unpredictable, which made the situation far more dangerous than usual.

The vamp tightened his hold on Miranda and Cody stepped forward, his fangs bared, his fury *this close* to simmering over.

"Fine." The vampire thrust her forward. "She's yours."

Cody caught Miranda and tucked her safely behind him.

Meanwhile, the young vamp turned his attention back to his first victim. "I've got my own."

"No," Miranda breathed, but her protest did little to stop the hungry vampire.

It was Cody's hand that caught him by the shoulder and brought him up short. "You won't make it another eight months if you keep being this stupid. All a vampire killer has to do is follow your trail of dead bodies and that'll be the end of you." Cody focused on the girl who lay sprawled in a fast-growing pool of her own blood. He could hear the faint beat of her heart and the slow draw of breath. She wasn't dead, but she was close. "You took too much blood. She'll live, but only if she gets medical attention right away." He spared the vampire a glance. "Take her to the hospital."

"Are you freakin' kidding me?"

Cody tightened his hold on the vampire. *"Take her to the hospital,"* he bit out. "Or you won't have to wait for the vampire killers to find you. I'll end your miserable existence myself."

"You wouldn't do that." The young vamp eyed him defiantly, but Cody didn't miss the flash of fear in the younger man's eyes. A few seconds ticked by and he seemed to deflate. "What the hell am I supposed to tell them?"

"You take her to the E.R., tell the front desk that you found her like this on the side of the road and then disappear. Don't give any names or locations. Just drop her off and leave."

The vamp nodded and scooped up the girl.

Cody watched the blur of shadows disappear before he turned toward Miranda. Her entire body shook and her lips trembled as she stared at the far end of the paved lot where the vamp had disappeared with the dying woman. A strange wave of possessiveness went through him and he stiffened.

"Miranda?"

At the sound of her name, her head snapped up and her gaze met his. Relief flashed before she seemed to remember what had just transpired and exactly what she'd seen.

The blood.

The fangs.

The truth.

"You." She stumbled backward, ramming her knee against a nearby car as she turned.

And then she bolted for her life.

Go, go, go, go, go, go, go!

The command echoed in Miranda's head as she dove behind the wheel, slammed and locked her car door and shoved the key in the ignition.

Panic zipped up and down her spine and her heart pounded so hard she thought it was going to burst out of her chest.

No, she told herself. *No, no, no, no, no.*

Vampires didn't exist.

But cold-blooded, psychotic killers did and that's who she'd stumbled upon. Maybe the guy *had* been drinking the woman's blood. But he was probably just some sick crazy. Or a cult member. Or a poor schmuck obsessed with the undead. That didn't make him an eight-month-old vampire.

It was the shock. She'd freaked at the sight of all that blood and so she'd imagined things. Like the growling and the fangs and the bloodred eyes.

No way had she really seen a *vampire,* much less two.

Cody's image rushed at her, his eyes a hot, bright red, his fangs bared. She shook her head. *No.*

It had been a trick of the light. A hallucination brought on by the trauma of facing death. Her own and the poor girl whose blood had spilled out onto the concrete.

Christ, she had to *do* something. Call someone.

Her brain raced as she revved the engine. She had her cell phone in her purse which she'd left in the glove compartment. Once she was a safe distance away, she could pull over and call 911. She shoved the car into reverse. Slamming her foot down, she stomped on the gas. The car jumped and swerved backward, tires screaming as loud as the denial in her head.

This couldn't be happening.

Her hands tingled and she glanced down at the sticky red that caked her own fingers. She could feel the trickle of blood from her neck where the man had nearly ripped her throat open before Cody had stopped him.

Cody had saved her.

Or so she'd thought. But then she'd seen the truth. The rage in his eyes. The vicious curl to his lips. The fangs.

No, no, no, no, no, no, no, no, no…

Fear clawed at her, threatening to choke her. She swallowed. Her hands tightened on the steering wheel and she pressed on the gas, maneuvering down the row and barely avoiding the tail end of a Lexus that hadn't pulled fully into its spot.

She hung a left at the far end of the row and found herself driving down another row. Her gaze bounced around, looking for a way out—

"*Easy.*"

The deep, masculine voice whispered through her head and her gaze snapped to the rearview mirror. She saw Cody standing in the middle of the lane several feet behind the car. His eyes gleamed a bright, brilliant blue.

Which made absolutely no sense because he had silver eyes. *Silver.*

A *vampire.*

The notion struck just as a loud whoosh echoed in her head. Her head snapped back around and just like that, he was standing on the pavement in front of her.

She slammed on the brakes. The car swerved around him. The right fender snagged an electric pole. The car lurched. The back-end slid around. Her forehead hit the steering wheel and pain exploded in her skull. A split second later, the airbag smacked her in the face, but not before she heard the driver's door open and saw the large, strong hands that reached for her.

Her head lolled to the side and she forced her eyes open despite the blinding pain. She caught a glimpse of dark hair and gleaming silver eyes.

Silver, she reminded herself. Not the blue she'd seen a few seconds ago. *Silver.*

And then the pressure in her skull overwhelmed her and she slipped into oblivion.

6

CODY PULLED MIRANDA out from under the air bag, opened the rear door and settled her on the soft leather. Other than the oozing prick-points at her neck, a cut on her forehead and some swelling, she seemed unharmed.

He turned to deal with the two security guards who'd heard the crash and barreled through the back door of the club.

"What the hell's going on?" The first guy's name was Joe and he was an Austin firefighter. He had a wife, two ex-wives and six kids, and so he moonlighted on the weekends as a bouncer. He had his cell in hand and was about to call in the accident when Cody turned his full attention on the man.

"Nothing," he said. The man looked ready to call the police anyway, but then his eyes glazed over and he nodded.

Cody went through the same spiel with bouncer number two.

Luckily, they were in the rear parking lot, which didn't have as much traffic as the one just across the street. A paid lot that offered security. The back lot was strictly for overflow and employees, so Cody didn't have to deal with anyone else coming out during the next few moments as he checked for damage to the car.

Other than a smashed right fender, everything else looked okay. He stuffed the air bag back into place, slid behind the wheel and flipped open the glove box. He retrieved her purse and found her wallet.

A glance at her driver's license and his stomach knotted.

Skull Creek.

The truth echoed in his head, along with a rush of dread because he'd just had the most incredible sex of his afterlife and now the plan was to gain as much distance as possible from the woman who'd given it to him.

He had a vampire to kill and a score to settle. He needed his concentration. His focus.

Shit.

Could his night get any worse?

A great big *Hell, yes!* smacked him upside the head when he pulled into the parking lot of a convenience store a short distance from the club and slid into the backseat to check on Miranda.

The place had long since closed and everything was dark, but he could see her anyway. Her smooth skin and full lips. The soft fan of her lashes on her cheeks. The swelling on her forehead was getting worse and Cody had the gut feeling that she had a concussion.

Shit.

He couldn't very well take her to a hospital and risk her gaining consciousness and blowing his cover to an entire E.R. full of doctors and nurses before he'd had a chance to mesmerize her and zap her memory. Not that they'd believe her, but the incredible story would surely stir some gossip and attention.

With Benny James on his heels, he couldn't afford either.

He had no choice but to help her himself.

Hesitation rushed through him. Ridiculous, of course. It wasn't like he was going to turn her into a vampire. She would have to be on her deathbed for that. Only if she drank some of his blood while dying would she become a vampire.

She was merely wounded, which meant his blood wouldn't turn her. It would only heal her, and strengthen the bond that already existed between them because of the sex.

He'd drank in her orgasm—her essence—which meant he could now feel her. If she drank his life-blood—his essence—she would be able to feel him, as well. His lust. His anger. His sorrow. His secrets. How strong those feelings would be, he wasn't sure. He'd never shared his blood with a human. He only knew the bond would become a two-way street.

Don't do it.

That's what reason told him, but his damned conscience whispered otherwise. He'd left her in that alley alone when he knew good and goddamn well that there was another vampire in the vicinity. Sure, he'd thought the young gun had taken off, but he should have sensed him still close by.

He would have if he hadn't been so freaked out by his own climax, and so damned desperate to get away.

To cut and run. Like always.

He focused on the hunger in his gut, letting it rise up and take control. His fangs sharpened and lengthened. Biting at his own wrist, he drew a steady drip-drop of blood. He held the wound to her lips and let the precious life trickle into her mouth.

He knew the moment her survival instincts kicked in. While her eyes didn't open, she arched up off the seat and grasped at his arm. Holding his wrist close, she lapped at his skin.

At the first feel of her tongue flicking against him, his groin tightened and his muscles went tense. She suckled, the drawing sensation sending a bolt of desire straight to his already aroused cock. He braced himself against the seat with his free hand and fought the urge to explode right there in his pants.

The agony went on several more seconds until he finally pulled away.

Her eyes opened then and she stared up at him. Her forehead wrinkled for a split second, but then he touched her. His fingertips trailed over her smooth skin, down the side of her face, her cheek and again he felt a surge of protectiveness.

Crazy. He wasn't doing this for her. This was about watching his own ass and covering his tracks. No police. No hospital.

He leaned down and lapped at the two tiny prick points at her neck. The taste hit him like a shot of whiskey, curling through him, stirring a wave of heat that warmed his insides and made him want more. His fangs sharpened and vibrated, but he resisted the draw of her sweet life. Instead, he laved the nicks with his tongue and forced himself away. His entire body trembled with the effort.

"Close your eyes and relax," he said, his voice gruff. "You'll be home soon."

She didn't want to, but he stared so hard into her gaze and impressed his will on her that she had no choice.

Stare into her eyes and will her to forget, a voice reminded him. *Erase her memory of you.* But damned if her eyelids didn't close before he had the chance.

At least, that's what he told himself.

Deep down, he knew the truth was that she'd come looking for a memory and he couldn't bring himself to rob her of it. It wasn't as if he could control exactly what she remembered. How far back. What specific events and episodes. Rather, he could make her forget him and all that that involved.

The sex.

The confrontation with the young vampire.

The accident.

The sharing of his blood.

The last thought stopped him cold. Since she'd tasted him, he might not be able to influence her thoughts and erase her memory. He didn't know.

Not that it mattered either way.

He'd erased the evidence and he had no doubt that she would convince herself that she hadn't really seen what she'd thought she'd seen. Reason and logic would win out over the truth. They always did.

He licked at his bleeding wrist before untucking his shirt and ripping off a strip from the bottom. He wrapped the cloth around the self-inflicted wound and tied a tight knot. The gash hurt like a sonofabitch and it looked even worse, but he knew the pain wouldn't last for long. A day of sleep and all traces of the injury would be completely gone.

For her, as well.

He slid off his shirt and draped it over her. Her heartbeat echoed in his head and his hands lingered on her smooth, warm cheek.

A quick second and he forced himself away.

And then he climbed behind the wheel, hit the interstate and headed for Skull Creek.

7

A NIGHTMARE.

That's what Miranda decided when she opened her eyes. She was stretched out in the backseat of her car parked in front of the two-story brick colonial she'd bought two years ago. Flower beds full of Texas sage and lantana lined the walkway to the front door and a well-tended ivy covered trellis decorated the right front of the house.

It was an older house and somewhat small, but it was well-kept and, more importantly, it was all hers. She'd scrimped and saved for years, living in a one-room efficiency over the local bakery and stashing every extra penny from her job at the senior center until she'd finally had enough for a down payment. Her sisters hadn't thought she'd be able to do it, but she had. Just as she'd put herself through college. And graduated at the top of her class.

The house, however, was her biggest accomplishment. Her pride and joy.

She'd refinished the kitchen cabinets and retiled the bathroom floor and she was now in the process of repainting her bedroom a creamy yellow with pale pink trim.

A far cry from the moldy, peeling papered walls of

the trailer where she'd grown up—where her sisters still lived—which was the point entirely. She'd wanted out of that life, and she'd made it.

Almost.

Relief threaded through her as she blinked against the blinding morning sunlight. A nightmare, all right, and now she was home. Safe.

She glanced at her hands just to be sure.

Sure enough, there wasn't a trace of blood anywhere. None on her clothes. Or the seat. She sat up and glanced in the rearview mirror. Other than a major case of bedhead, she looked the way she always did. No bleeding cuts or bruises. Nothing but the smooth, slightly pale skin of her forehead.

She was *never* drinking again. Or having hot, wild sex with a vampire.

Her thighs trembled and her thoughts careened to a halt.

Wait a second.

A vampire?

Hardly. Vampires didn't exist. Only in the minds of cable TV producers, ambitious horror writers and women hung up on the ultimate alpha male fantasy.

Her mother had liked vampires almost as much as she'd liked cowboys. She'd lusted over Brad Pitt in *Interview with the Vampire* until she'd practically worn out the DVD.

They were the stuff of fantasies, all right. As in fake. Fictitious. *Un*real.

She remembered Cody's hot mouth on her nipple and the nub tightened. Her thighs still tingled from the rough feel of his hands.

Real.

The sex, that is. But then she'd crawled into the backseat of her car and passed out, and dreamt up all the rest.

So how the hell had she gotten home?

A good Samaritan, obviously. She'd been in no condition to drive, which meant some do-gooder had happened along and given her a lift. That, or maybe one of the bouncers had played chauffeur. Or maybe a tow truck had hauled her home. Or…something. Anything. Because no way had last night actually happened.

Cody the cowboy *vampire* had been just a figment of her imagination. A margarita-induced hallucination. And now it was over.

She gathered her resolve and climbed from the car. For having tied one on—they must have let the worm through when they poured the tequila for her margarita—she actually felt pretty good. No lingering headache or nausea. Just an ache between her thighs that reminded her of the most glorious orgasm of her entire life.

She'd really and truly done it.

Finally.

She did her damnedest to resist the smile that tugged at her lips. Grabbing her purse from the front seat, she walked around the car to pick up her newspaper. She was just straightening when she spotted the twisted front right fender. A memory rushed at her and she felt the wheel beneath her fingers, the jolt as the car hit the light pole, the explosion of pain in her skull.

Her gaze skittered a few feet and snagged on the western shirt draped over her mailbox. Her heart started to pound and her mind rushed back. She felt the soft cotton slithering over her arms, smelled the mesmerizing scent of leather and wildness and raw power.

No way.

No. Friggin'. *Way.*

He wasn't a vampire. He couldn't be. That much she knew. As for driving her home… Maybe he *had* been the one to drive her here.

Maybe he was still here.

Yeah, right.

If—and we're talking a big *if* considering there were a dozen other possibilities—he *had* driven her home, he was nowhere in sight now. A quick glance inside the car confirmed what she already knew—no note. No good-bye. Nothing.

She snatched up the shirt, walked toward her front door and tried to ignore a crazy rush of disappointment.

She'd hooked up with him precisely because he wasn't the type of man who stuck around for an awkward morning after.

One wild night, she reminded herself.

And now it was back to her calm, tame life.

"I AIN'T NEVER SEEN a shopping cart do this much damage." Darrell Call ran one grease-stained hand over the twisted metal.

He was the owner and operator of Darrell's Pit Stop, probably the last full service gas station in the free world. While he wasn't actually open on Sundays, she'd caught him in his garage doing an oil change on old man Witherspoon's 1970 Bonneville.

"Are you sure that's all you hit?" he finally asked after another careful inspection.

Miranda shrugged. "It might have been two of them stuck together." She'd gone to high school with Darrell. He'd been one of the only boys who hadn't hit on her—he'd only had eyes for Mabel Sinclair. They'd married right after high school and had three kids—Little Darrel, May and Ranger—named after Darrell's favorite baseball team.

"My cousin rammed a shopping cart once." Darrell let loose a stream of tobacco juice and arched an eyebrow at her. "All he got was a few little scratches."

"They're making them sturdier these days."

"They painting 'em yellow, too?" He eyeballed a small section that had flecks of dried paint embedded in the metal.

"I might have grazed one of those parking posts after I hit the shopping cart. Can you fix it?" she added before he could ask another question.

He shrugged. "I can try banging her out, but if that don't work I'll have to order a new fender."

"How long do you think it will take?"

"A week or two. Maybe more. Depends on if we have to order parts."

Dread welled inside her. The last thing she wanted was to have to explain the car to anyone.

She didn't want to lie.

She never lied. Her mother had been a master at it. She'd explained away her daughters to the men she'd brought home, calling them everything from her nieces to her younger sisters.

"I really need this car back as soon as possible."

Darrell adjusted his ball cap and shook his head. "You cain't hurry skilled craftsmanship."

"I'll pay extra."

"You and the half dozen car owners in front of you. I'm the only mechanic in town. I've got me one of them monopolies going on."

"Free movie tickets?"

"I already got a whole mess of tickets from Myron Haskell over at the theater. I helped him restore his '69 GTO."

"We've got pay-per-view at the senior center." She wiggled her eyebrows. "I'll spring for wrestling tomorrow night."

"Got my own satellite dish. Fixed Diane Holloway's Plymouth last year and she gave it to me."

Diane owned the mercantile that sold everything from big screens to zit cream.

"I'll mow your lawn."

"That's Mabel's area. She says it helps to keep her ass from spreading on account of she sits all day. She's on a health kick. Can you believe she made me get rid of the snack machines in the office? I tried to buy a chili dog over at the diner last week and Sue Jean refused to sell it to me. Said Mabel told her to cut me off or else. I cain't even buy a Snickers bar at the Quick Pick."

An idea struck and Miranda contemplated Mabel's wrath all of five seconds before she made up her mind. "I *could* bring you a dozen Krispy Kremes from the senior center." Hey, desperate times called for desperate measures. "We get a fresh shipment every morning."

He grinned. "Sugar *does* make me work faster."

Miranda vowed to deliver donuts first thing the next morning and headed to the local nursery to pick up a bag of potting soil.

It was her usual Sunday morning trip.

She walked her normal route and stopped off at the bakery for her favorite bagel. She said hello to the busy-bodies drinking coffee in front of the diner the way she always did and they *harrumphed* and *why, I nevered* the way they always did. It was the same old, same old in Skull Creek.

Except that it didn't feel like the same old.

It felt different this time.

She felt different.

Her heart beat a little faster. Her body felt more alert. Her ears perked at the slightest sound and her finger-tips tingled. Her nose seemed more sensitive, picking up the sweet smell of cotton candy even though she was a block away from the carnival being held in the church parking lot.

And her eyes… She noticed colors that she'd never noticed before. The different shades of red in the single rose that bloomed in a pot on her back patio. The iridescent aqua wings on the fly that buzzed around her kitchen.

She felt different, all right.

Alive.

Thanks to Cody.

She dismissed the absurd thought as she pulled on her gardening gloves and went to work on the flower beds in her backyard.

She and Greg had started the planting just last month.

He loved flowers and spent every second when he wasn't running the dry cleaning business tending a greenhouse full of prizewinning daisies. Miranda herself had never been into gardening until he'd bought her a pair of gloves and put her to work.

Now she shared his routine even if she didn't share his passion.

Wait a second.

Who said she didn't share his passion? Sure, she wasn't a fanatic about it, but she *liked* gardening.

Seeing a mound of dirt transform into a brilliant cluster of flowers filled her with a sense of pride. And hope. If she could change her surroundings, she could change her life.

She most certainly wasn't letting herself get hung up on a one-night-stand with a virtual stranger. No matter how phenomenal the orgasm. Or how she kept reliving the memory of the two of them in that back alley. Or how she kept envisioning them getting hot and heavy in the front loader of a John Deere tractor. Or buck-naked on the fifty-yard line at the local stadium. Or sweaty and desperate in the back seat of her car—

Enough!

She wasn't thinking about him. And she certainly wasn't thinking about the *Sex Spots* List. Sure, she'd wondered in the past what it might be like to do it in the various locations—she was only human, after all— but she'd never pictured herself with any certain someone.

Until now.

Over, she reminded herself. Her head knew that.

If only her hormones could grasp that all-important fact.

8

SHE WAS THINKING ABOUT HIM.

Fantasizing.

Wanting.

The realization peeled back the edges of sleep and slithered down under the covers with him. Desire burned into Cody like a cattle brand as he found himself pulled into her fantasy.

They were smack dab in the middle of Town Square in a small, white gazebo. He peeled off his clothes and she peeled off hers, both of them oblivious to the occasional car that zipped up Main Street. That was half the fun. The spurt of excitement when they heard the grumble of an engine. The fear of discovery. The excitement.

His cock throbbed and he touched himself, stroking his length and mimicking the movement of her hand. He kissed her with all the desperation building in his body before she pulled away and slid down between his legs. Her mouth closed over the head of his erection. She licked, swirling her tongue and driving him crazy before sucking him deep into her mouth.

His fingers closed in her silky hair, holding her close as he bucked his hips and urged himself deeper into the wet heat of her mouth. She sucked. The back of her throat rasped the head of his penis. His fingers tightened. His body went stiff and he exploded—

Cody's eyes snapped open to find his hands clenched in the sheets and his body trembling.

He glanced at the digital alarm clock sitting on the scarred nightstand. It was barely noon. The truth registered and disbelief rushed through him. He didn't wake up in the middle of the day. And he certainly didn't have wet dreams. He was a vampire, for Christ's sake. When he slept, he *slept*. There was no tossing and turning and dreaming. And he sure as hell did *not* jack-off.

He threw off the sheet and wiped at his gritty eyes. A bright yellow glow outlined the edges of the blinds and made a criss-cross pattern across the hardwood floor. He spared a glance at the door. The deadbolt was turned, still locked tight. A chair wedged under the door just in case the *Do Not Disturb* sign wasn't enough to keep out the cleaning staff. Or, in this case, a nosy old woman who'd already warned him about tracking in mud.

Her name was Winona Adkins. She was an ancient lady with snow-white hair, glasses and white orthopedic shoes. She ran the town's one and only motel with her grandson, Eldin. He handled the lobby area while she puttered around, cleaning rooms and handing out extra towels.

It wasn't the type of place where Cody usually hung his hat. He liked his privacy and he sure as hell didn't like the twenty questions directed at him when he'd checked in just minutes before daybreak.

Thanks to his preternatural speed, he'd made it to and from Austin to pick up his truck in record time. Still, he'd cut it close. The fanfare when he'd pulled out his driver's license—who knew Eldin watched bullriding?—had delayed him even longer.

Cody had gotten stuck signing a dozen autographs just to get his room key.

"I'm taking a little breather before I get back on the road," he'd told the man to explain his sudden appearance in town. "You know how it is."

"Don't you worry, Mr. Boyd. We get celebrities in here all the time and I know just what to do. Why, I had me a fancy reporter here not very long ago. Name was Viv Darland and she wrote for some hotshot tabloid out in Hollywood. I kept the jackals away from her, you can best be sure. And if things get to out of hand, I can always call in the big guns. Sheriff Keller's new in town, but he's good."

After escorting Cody to the one and only room in the motel that had its own toilet and shower, he'd pulled out a lounge chair and a BB gun and parked himself out on the walkway in front of Cody's door.

Meanwhile, Winona had gotten on the phone and called someone named Gladys who'd called someone name Cheryl who'd called someone named Myrtle and so on.

Hence the chair wedged under the door and the lamp perched precariously on top. If the chair budged, the lamp would shatter and Cody would be awake in an instant.

Tired, but awake.

That's the way it was for vamps during the day. It wasn't that they couldn't open their eyes. The daylight drained their strength and made them vulnerable. Which was why they opted to sleep during that time.

That, and the sunlight, of course. Talk about a bitch to the complexion.

All the more reason to burrow deeper under the covers, away from the shafts of light pushing past the blinds, close his eyes and forget everything. He needed to rest. To regenerate. Particularly after offering up some of his precious energy to Miranda.

She'd drank his blood and he'd drank the sweet energy of her climax, and the damage was done. They were linked now.

The truth vibrated through him along with a swirl of emotions—her emotions. She felt everything from disbelief to anxiety to desperation as she tried to justify what had happened and come up with a plausible story that didn't shake the foundation of her beliefs.

A vampire?

Insane. Impossible.

She fought the truth just as he fought the damned connection to her.

He focused on the steady *whirrrr* of the air conditioner. The drip-drop of water from the bathroom sink. The groaning of the lounge chair as Eldin abandoned his post to go in search of a bag of Doritos and a strawberry Crush.

As the outside world slipped into his head, Cody managed to ignore the constant buzz of her emotions and stop thinking about her.

For a little while.

Until he closed his eyes and found himself remembering the past night. How warm she'd felt. How wet. How eager. She'd been that way from the very beginning with no influence from him. One glance and she'd wanted him.

He'd never encountered that before. True, he had dozens of buckle bunnies vying for his attention, but none of them really and truly wanted *him.* Cody Braddock. They were more interested in the infamous Cody Boyd. His fame. His money. That's what gave them the courage to walk over to him. The lust didn't hit until he stared deep into their eyes and mesmerized them with his vamp charm. Only then did they want to peel off their panties and climb into the saddle for a nice, long ride.

Not Miranda. She'd wanted him at first glance, *before* he'd worked any of his vamp mojo on her.

She still wanted him.

He knew the feeling.

The minute the thought struck, he sprawled onto his back and stared at the ceiling. His body throbbed and his cock bobbed, pushing against the crisp cotton sheet. A quick brush of his fingertips on the hard shaft and desire bolted through him. His stomach hollowed out. His fangs tingled.

Maybe he wasn't feeling her so much as wanting her. He'd shared his blood with her last night, which made him at least a pint shy. He was weak again. Hungry.

The hunger.

That's what had him tossing and turning and thinking that going back for seconds might not be such a bad thing. He needed all of his strength when he confronted Garret Sawyer and made him pay for his sins.

It sure as hell wasn't because Miranda had felt different from any other woman he'd ever been with— hotter, wetter, wilder. Or because she'd stared up at him for those few seconds when he'd saved her from that young greedy vampire as if he were some kind of white knight instead of the devil himself.

No woman had ever seen the good in him. Except his mother, of course. No matter what bad thing he'd done, she'd dismissed it with a wink and a "You know how boys are," or "He's the baby of the bunch."

He could still remember the way she'd stared up at him that tragic night, her eyes bright with love and hope.

As if he'd ridden up in time to save the day.

But he hadn't been anyone's hero that night. And he sure as hell wasn't one now. He was something much darker and a hell of a lot more dangerous.

Miranda knew that and she still wanted him.

The truth haunted him for the rest of the day as he tried to rest and rejuvenate and forget about the fact that she was thinking about him.

And the sex.

And how he'd helped her cross one location off her *Hot Spots* List.

And how he'd protected her after the fact and covered her up with that damned shirt.

He never should have left it.

It had been a moment of impulse. A crazy burst of ego that had kicked his common sense to the curb. It was better for her to reason it all away and convince herself nothing out of the ordinary had happened. He'd known that, but deep down inside, he hadn't wanted her to reason him away.

He wanted to live on in her thoughts long after she made the biggest mistake of her life and married the wrong man.

He knew that just as he knew that she wasn't half as sure about Mr. Right as she should have been, otherwise she never would have been in that club in the first place.

Not that doubt was going to stop her. She was determined. Marriage. House with the white picket fence and the minivan and a couple of kids to distract her from the demons that pushed and pulled inside of her. The ones she'd unleashed last night for a precious few moments when she'd been with him.

She'd bottled it all back up inside now. She was now working in her garden and going through the motions and pretending that last night had never happened.

Exactly what he intended to do. They were over and done with. Finished.

Even if he was desperately hungry and she'd given him a burst of strength unlike any he'd ever felt before.

He'd get the same rush from anyone else.

That's what he told himself when he finally hauled his ass out of bed at sunset.

Even more, he intended to prove it.

He grabbed his hat and headed for the bar and grill he'd passed on his way into town.

A quick lay, some sweet, energizing sex, and then he could get on with the business of killing Garret Sawyer.

9

CODY MEANT TO HEAD STRAIGHT for the bar and grill, but instead found himself standing in front of Skull Creek's one and only custom motorcycle shop.

Sweet, sweet revenge.

That was the reason he'd come here first. He'd waited a long time to confront his family's killer and he wasn't about to waste another second, even if he was weaker than he would have liked. He needed to lay the past to rest. He couldn't change what happened that night, but he could make sure that Garret Sawyer never murdered again.

He could do something now when he'd been too late to do something then.

Shadows gathered around him as he stared up at the front of the building.

Other than the neon blue *Home of Skull Creek Choppers* that hummed in the front window and the hi-tech security pad that sat next to the entrance, the place looked like Mayberry.

The building was an old fifties service station complete with antique gas pumps and an orange and white Davey's Fill-r-Up ball that rotated atop an iron pole. An ancient soda machine filled with glass bottles sat to the left of the front windows. Old-fashioned signs for everything from Goo Goo Clusters to Husky Motor Oil hung here and there.

His vision sharpened as he stared through the front windows. The inside had been turned into an office area complete with several large filing cabinets and an impressive computer system. Framed pictures of various custom-made choppers lined the wall along with a DBA certificate and a sales tax permit. Behind the computer system stood another wall of windows that overlooked the actual machine shop.

Fluorescent lights blazed overhead, illuminating several stainless steel work tables and the bare bones frame of a current work in progress. An industrial strength welding unit sat nearby, along with a large grinder, several sprayers and an impressive assortment of tools that lined the walls. An array of saw blades covered one twelve-foot surface.

It looked like an average machine shop, not the hideout of a vicious, murdering vampire. Doubt niggled at Cody and stirred the one question that still remained unanswered about that night.

If Garret Sawyer had slaughtered the women and children and set the ranch on fire to cover his tracks after his feeding frenzy, then why hadn't Sawyer done the same thing to the brothers? Why had he turned them instead?

Because he's a ruthless, unpredictable, bloodthirsty vampire, Cody told himself for the countless time. *He was there. Covered in blood. With the murder weapon in his hand. He's guilty, all right.*

Probably.

Cody ignored the last thought and concentrated on the sounds drifting from inside.

"If you don't hurry up, they're going to leave without us," a soft, feminine voice said.

"Maybe that's not such a bad thing," came the deep reply.

A door creaked open somewhere and Cody felt a rush of tingling awareness. His muscles clenched and his gut tightened and he barely resisted the urge to put his fist through the glass and barrel in.

But there was a woman inside.

While Cody had every intention of ripping out Garret Sawyer's black heart, he wasn't losing control and taking out an innocent bystander.

"You've got a one-track brain," the woman declared.

"You act like that's a bad thing."

"Actually," the woman purred, "it's a very good thing. It's just that I've been wanting to see this movie for over three months…"

Cody blinked frantically against the red clouding his vision. A hundred years of regret had twisted and morphed into a living breathing monster even more vicious than the bloodlust.

Garret Sawyer had robbed him of his mother. His memories. And for that he would pay.

Cody hit the buzzer that sat next to the high-tech keypad and braced himself.

Immediately he felt the tension that rushed through the vampire inside as he became aware of another presence. A hiss sizzled through the air.

A split second later, a tall, muscular form appeared

in the doorway that separated the office from the machine shop. He wore blue jeans, a button-down black shirt that clung to his broad torso and a worn pair of cowboy boots. He had shoulder-length brown hair that had been pulled back into a ponytail. Red rimmed his dark pupils. The tips of his fangs gleamed in the fading dusk.

He was a vampire, all right.

But he wasn't *the* vampire that haunted Cody's memories.

"Yeah?" the vamp asked. "What can I do you for?"

"I'm looking for Garret Sawyer."

"Why?"

Cody tamped down on the anger swirling inside him. "I'm an old friend. I saw his picture in a recent magazine and I thought I'd stop by to catch up." It was part-truth and part-lie, but the vampire didn't need to know that.

Vampires couldn't read other vampires which made trust nearly impossible.

A vampire had to rely on his gut instincts when it came to those of his kind, and this one could obviously sense that Cody wanted more than to reminisce.

His eyes still glowed and his fangs still glittered and his entire body seemed poised, as if he waited for an attack. "Are you interested in a bike? If so, I can help you. I'm Jake McCann. I handle all the designs for Skull Creek Choppers."

"I'm not here for a bike."

"Then what do you want with Garret?"

"Jake? I didn't realize you had an appointment." The

voluptuous blonde came up short as she reached the doorway. Jake stepped in front of her, tucking her safely behind him as he faced off with Cody.

"Honey?" The female's hand touched Jake's arm. "What's going on?"

He covered her fingers with his own and gave her an affectionate squeeze. "Nothing. This guy thought he had a meeting with Garret tonight, but he obviously made a mistake." His gaze collided with Cody's. "Right?"

Cody ignored the vampire and caught the gaze of the woman. Not that he expected to read her thoughts. She was a vampire. But sometimes with newly turned vamps he could pick up at least an impression or two.

She was definitely a babe in the woods. Otherwise, she would have sensed the threat that he posed.

Even so, he couldn't catch even a glimpse of her thoughts.

"She's used to nosy vampires." Jake's deep voice drew his attention.

"I live with one," she added. Affection filled her voice as she slid an arm around Jake's waist and regarded Cody with suspicious eyes. "I can block better than a Dallas Cowboys defensive lineman."

"Where can I find Sawyer?" Cody pressed. When neither vampire replied, he added, "It's not privileged information. Not in a small town like this." He smiled, an easy, relaxed expression that contradicted the tense set of his muscles. "You know as well as I do that I can find him if I really want to."

"Garret's out of town on business," Jake said after a long contemplative moment. "He flew out last night."

"When is he coming back?"

The vampire didn't look as if he wanted to answer. Instead he stared, as if he looked hard enough, he might be able to see what Cody had in mind. "Friday," he finally said.

It wasn't the news Cody had hoped for. It was only Sunday. He would have to stick around for five full days.

At the same time, he'd spent an afterlife waiting for this moment. Five days meant nothing. If anything, it would give him time to gather his strength. He would need it judging by the defiant vampires in front of them. They would stand by Garret.

Which meant that Cody needed to feed.

A lot.

He had a sudden vision of Miranda, her pale skin gleaming in the moonlight, her essence drenching his cock as he pumped inside of her. A growl vibrated up his throat.

Jake's survival skills kicked in at the sound and his lips pulled back. His fangs glittered.

"Easy." Cody threw up his hands. "I've got no beef with you. It's your friend I'm after." He tamped down on the tightening in his gut and gathered his control. "Tell Sawyer I'm coming for him."

"What do you want with him?" the female asked.

"IRS." Cody winked. "Your buddy owes a shitload and I'm here to collect." He tipped his hat. "Sorry to keep you from your movie, ma'am." And then he turned on his heel and walked away.

Five days.

Shit.

His insides clenched and his hunger stirred as he left Skull Creek Choppers and headed down Main Street. He meant to head for the nearest bar, but instead of going east, he found himself headed the opposite direction. To a small two-story house with a yard full of flowers.

Not that he was going to feed off Miranda. And make the connection that much stronger? Hell, no. Rather, he was going to do his damnedest to erase her memory. It might not work. It probably wouldn't work, but he had to try. If he succeeded, then she would stop thinking about him. Then maybe, just maybe, he could stop thinking about her and keep his distance for the next few days.

Otherwise…

He ignored the lustful thought that slammed into him and picked up his steps. He was ending this.

Now.

10

THE LOUD *DINGGGG DONGGGG* echoed in Miranda's head and her hand stalled on the lid of a mayonnaise jar.

A strange tingling swept through her, part fear, part excitement. Suddenly she didn't know whether to answer the door or run like hell.

It was him.

She felt it in the way her nipples tightened and her legs trembled. Her stomach hollowed out and her heart went into overdrive.

Yeah, right.

It could be anyone at her front door.

Mrs. Barthels from next door. The woman loved to stop by and gripe about *something*. Miranda's rose bushes were too high. Her patio lights were too bright. Her sprinklers were too noisy.

Little Jenna McGhee. She was a Girl Scout and cookie season had just started.

Mr. Bonney. He'd been trying to sell her tickets to the VFW barbecue since last week.

Claire Jackson. Whenever her no-good husband Cal didn't come home, she always went looking for him. She'd caught Cal with Miranda's older sister, Lucy, only once. But that was all it had taken to throw a veil of suspicion on Miranda herself. She was a Rivers, after all. Translation? Trashy and no good. No man was safe and so whenever Cal came up missing, Claire always paid Miranda a very unpleasant visit.

That would stop if she married Greg.

If?

There was no *if*. She was marrying him.

The doorbell rang again before she could worry over the doubt that whispered through her. She gathered her control and set the mayonnaise jar to the side.

It wasn't Cody, and there was one way to prove it.

She made it three steps before the back door flew open. Shock bolted through Miranda and she whirled as a tall, leggy redhead waltzed in.

Lucy Rivers was just two years older than Miranda, but too many nights of drinking and smoking made it seem more like ten. The wear and tear dulled her bright blue eyes just enough to give her that jaded look. However worn and worldly, she was still a beautiful girl. She had an hourglass figure that would have made even Jessica Simpson envious, and long, silky hair that flowed to her waist.

With the right clothes, she could have looked like a runway model. Instead, she looked like any other barmaid down at the Iron Horse. She wore the standard uniform—a pair of Daisy Duke shorts, red cowboy boots and a Hawaiian print tube top. Bright red lipstick colored her full mouth and heavy black pencil rimmed her blue eyes.

"What's up, Randy?"

"Geez, you scared the crap out of me." Miranda drew

a deep breath. "I thought you were at the front door." She glanced down the hallway, but there wasn't so much as a shadow on the other side of the oval glass that sat in the middle of the door.

"Why wait around when I know you leave the back door unlocked? Besides, we're family. What's yours is mine. *Mi casa, su casa. Mi sandwich, su sandwich.*" She grinned and picked up the turkey and Swiss Miranda had just made.

"Wait—" Miranda started, but Lucy's mouth had already closed over the corner.

She took a huge bite and chewed. "Kudos, Sis. You make one hell of a sandwich. I'm terrible with cooking."

"It's a sandwich. It's pretty much foolproof if you've got the stuff."

"Which you always have because you do grocery shopping so much better than me."

"You don't do grocery shopping, period."

She wiggled her eyebrows. "I do grocery clerks. That cute one that works on Friday evenings and that new guy that just started full-time."

"That's not what I meant."

"I know. I just like to watch you turn red. You're such a goody goody. I bet you've never tried anything other than the missionary position."

Her palms itched at the memory of her hands pressed to the brick and Cody behind her. If only Lucy knew.

"I would really appreciate it if we could talk about something else." Miranda blew out a breath and made a beeline for the fridge. Pulling out a Diet Coke, she lingered a split second and let the rush of cool air soothe her cheeks before snagging an extra drink for her sister.

She shut the refrigerator door to find her sister eyeing her, an amused grin tugging at her lips.

"Speaking of missionary, how *is* Mr. Tight Ass?"

"He's great."

"Really? You'd never know it to look at him. Big penis?"

"I didn't mean in bed. I meant in general."

"I know." Lucy grinned and headed for the pantry and a box of cupcakes. "Don't you ever buy Twinkies? Chocolate makes me break out."

"So what do you want?" Miranda asked. "Besides food, that is."

"Who says I want anything? Maybe I'm just here to bond with my little sister." Miranda gave her a *yeah, right* look and she added, "Okay, so maybe I could use twenty bucks. There's this new bar that just opened up over in Cherry Creek. I thought I'd drive over after I finished my shift tonight and see if there are any hot guys hanging out."

"Use your tip money."

"Are you kidding? The only regulars that come in on Sunday night are Earl Kinley and his poker buddies."

"So?"

"So they play for gum. The only thing I pick up on a Sunday night is a few packs of Hubba Bubba and the occasional piece of Dentyne. That won't pay a cover charge, let alone buy any drinks."

"You *could* go home and call it a night," Miranda asked hopefully. "Maybe read a book. Or watch TV."

"Or listen to my arteries hardening," Lucy added. "No, thank you. I'd rather meet a hot cowboy."

"You already know more than enough."

"There's no such thing when it comes to the opposite sex." She finished off the cupcake and grabbed an apple from a nearby fruit bowl. "So are you going to give me the twenty bucks, or what?"

"What if I say no?"

"You won't."

"Why not?"

"Because I'll pay you back."

"You never pay me back."

"Yeah, well." She shrugged. "I don't have as great a job as you."

"You could change that if you went back to school."

"You know I don't do school." Lucy grabbed her soda and the rest of the sandwich. "If you don't want to lend me the money, I'll figure something else out. I heard about this girl who put her used panties on eBay and made fifty bucks. Or I could offer blow jobs. Or sell my soul to the devil—"

"I'll give you the twenty bucks," Miranda cut in. "But you're paying me back this time."

"Sure thing."

"I mean it." Miranda retrieved her purse and pulled a bill from her wallet.

"Gotcha." Lucy grabbed the money and a banana for the road. "I'll call you tomorrow and we can catch up," she added and then disappeared through the back door.

But Lucy Rivers never called just to catch up. The only time she dialed Miranda or stopped by was when she wanted something. Money. Food. A place to stay because whatever guy she'd been crashing with had kicked her out.

Just like their oldest sister Robin.

Robin Rivers had the same shameless attitude even if it was wrapped up in an entirely different package. She had dark brown hair, green eyes and the sharp, poignant features of her Cherokee father.

At least that's what their mother had always said.

Robin was currently playing groupie to a local country band touring the southwest. She'd laid everyone in the band with the exception of the drummer. A situation she had every intention of changing before they pulled back into town in a few months.

She'd called three weeks ago to announce she'd just gotten it on with the lead singer after a round of quarters and enough tequila to pickle a horse. After the announcement, she'd talked Miranda into sending her one hundred dollars to buy some new spandex and see her through the end of the tour, and that had been the end of their conversation.

Not that she wanted Robin to call just to talk. Or Lucy either, for that matter. The last thing she needed was a real relationship with either of her sisters. It was hard enough convincing the world she'd changed. Keeping company with two of the most notorious bad girls in town would only undo all of her hard work.

Still…

Sometimes she couldn't help but wonder what it would be like to go shopping once in a while or have lunch or sit through an all-night gab fest like normal sisters.

She ignored the thought and headed outside to put away her gardening tools. She'd been so desperate to forget Cody that she'd worked like a demon. All she had to do now was sprinkle some growth pellets and she was finished—

Her thoughts stalled as awareness skittered up her spine. The scent of leather and wildness teased her nostrils. Her heart paused and her entire body went on high alert. She knew then that it wasn't just her wishful thinking.

Cody Braddock stood right behind her.

A frantic heartbeat later, his deep, husky, "Long time, no see," confirmed it.

_11_

HE LOOKED EVEN BETTER than she remembered.

Her porch light gleamed behind him, outlining his broad shoulders and muscular arms. He should have seemed more shadow than man, but he didn't.

Despite the black Stetson that sat low on his forehead, shrouding his face and giving him a dangerous edge, she could still see every detail. His unique silver eyes framed with thick black lashes. The scar that zig-zagged across his cheek. The sensual set of his mouth. The faint stubble that surrounded his mouth and crept down his corded neck.

He wore a black T-shirt that clung to his solid chest and sported the PBR emblem, faded blue jeans that cupped his crotch and molded to his muscular thighs, and the same worn boots he'd had on last night.

Her stomach hollowed out and need shook her.

Fierce.

Intense.

Crazy.

Because Miranda didn't have a thing for cowboys. A mild infatuation, she reminded herself. One she'd satisfied last night.

Even so, her heartbeat kicked up a notch and her

breath caught and for the first time in her life, she couldn't help but sympathize with her mother and her damning weakness for cowboys. They *were* potent. Particularly this one.

Not that Miranda was giving in. While she'd pretended last night, she *wasn't* Restroom Randy. Nix the bad girl who paraded around in a pair of pink cowboy boots, picking up strange men and having hot sex in alleys.

She'd never even worn the boots until last night.

And she made it a point never to strut.

And she certainly didn't pick up men. Or have hot sex. Even with Greg.

Especially with Greg.

She ignored the depressing thought and fought down the urge to lead Cody around the house, steer him toward the swing that hung from her front porch—number six on the list—and mark off yet another location.

She gave herself a great big kick in the butt and braced herself against the lust bubbling inside her. The hope. "I thought you went back to Austin."

"You thought wrong. I had business in town, so here I am."

"Here?"

He nodded.

"In *this* town?"

Another nod.

Talk about rotten luck. She'd driven two hours to Austin just to make sure that she didn't run into anyone she knew. All so that she could pick up the one guy headed straight for her home town. "So why didn't you tell me that last night?"

"You didn't ask." His eyes took on a smoldering light. "You weren't exactly in the mood to talk."

"Just for the record," she blurted, a lifetime of denial raging inside of her. "I don't usually go to places like that. Or have sex with men."

He arched an interested eyebrow. "So you have sex with women?"

"Of course not. I have sex with men. That is, I've *had* sex with men. Three," the words seemed to tumble out of their own accord, each one stumbling over the other. "Not at the same time, of course. Three over the past ten years. They were old boyfriends. First there was Ronnie back in high school. Then Jimmy. Then Greg."

"Then me. That makes four, right?"

"I'm getting married," she blurted, desperately trying to get to the point. "To Greg. He's a really great guy. He owns Dynamite Drycleaning."

"Don't most engaged women start hunting for wedding invitations instead of one night stands?"

"I'm not actually engaged. Not yet. He asked, but I haven't said yes. He's out of town right now and he sent me an e-mail, but I don't want to e-mail the answer. Not that I don't want to marry him. I definitely do and I will. Last night was just…" She shook her head. "I just wanted to know what it felt like."

"To sleep with a strange man?"

To have an orgasm with any man. It was there. On the tip of her tongue. But she already had the feeling he knew more about her than she cared to admit and so she kept that to herself. She shrugged. "To have a little fun. You know, noncommittal, no strings attached, no awkward morning after before I commit myself and take the plunge. I've never done anything like that so it stands to reason that I would be curious. Any woman would."

"And?"

"And what?"

He arched an eyebrow. "How did it feel?"

"Fine. That is, up until the part where you grew fangs." It was a ridiculous thing to say which was exactly why she'd said it. He'd tell her she'd had one too many drinks and kill the lingering doubt that wiggled around deep down inside.

No way was he a bona fide *vampire*.

The sex. That's what had her so loopy. The orgasm had been so incredible it had short-circuited her brain cells.

She *knew* that.

"What happened last night?" she heard herself ask anyway.

He stared at her for a long moment, into her before he finally murmured, "Don't you know?"

"I know what happened between us." The kissing. The touching. The bone-melting one-on-one. Her cheeks flamed at the thought and she fought down a wave of heat. "I'm talking about after that." Her gaze met his and suddenly it all seemed too incredible. "You're just a man," she told him, as if saying the words would make them true.

He sized her up, his gaze pushing deep and prodding at her secrets. "That's what you say, but that's not what you really believe." He touched a fingertip between her breasts. "Not here. Here you know the truth. You know what I am." His eyes brightened and her breath caught.

"A man," she insisted. "Flesh and blood. Real."

If only.

Cody stiffened at the thought.

Sure, he'd earned a reputation and a lot of fame, but none of that made up for what he'd lost. His humanity. His life. The only time he felt truly alive was when he climbed on the bull.

Which was why he fully intended to hang on for another season despite Benny James.

He needed those eight seconds. He craved it.

The danger. The ride.

That was *living*.

The day-to-day grind that most people called a life seemed more like a death sentence to Cody. No excitement. No oomph.

He glanced at the perfectly kept yard and he knew that that was exactly the type of existence Miranda had carved out for herself.

Nice. Predictable. Safe.

None of it fit with the woman he'd met last night.

"You look different," the words were out before he could stop them. Gone was the blonde bombshell who'd been out looking for a one night stand. Her long pale hair was pulled back into a neat ponytail. She wore very little makeup with only a hint of lip gloss to accent her full lips. A loose white T-shirt covered her luscious breasts and a pair of baggy shorts did little to accent her soft, round ass. Dirt-caked tennis shoes completed the outfit. The only thing that even hinted that she was the same bombshell was the desire that sparked when her gaze met his. He noted her pink cheeks and healthy color and knew her injuries had healed completely.

Thanks to him.

His groin tightened at the memory of her drawing on his vein. He'd drank from plenty of women, but he'd never given and he couldn't shake the feel of her mouth, her tongue grazing his flesh, her lips sucking greedily.

He stiffened, fighting down the hunger that raged up and tightened his muscles. As much as he'd liked it, he wasn't letting it happen again.

He was here to weaken the connection, not make it that much stronger.

He stared deep into her eyes, focused his energy and willed her to forget. *Now.*

"It was a trick of the light," she pressed and he knew then that mesmerizing her would be impossible. She was stronger now because of his blood.

As disappointed as he was, he couldn't stifle the tiny spurt of joy that went through him. A feeling that made him all the more determined to do *something* to break the bond between them.

He needed her to stop wanting him.

"You didn't really," she went on, licking her lips again, "that is, you don't actually have *fangs.*"

She didn't want to believe he was something straight out of a nightmare. No one did. They were scared to believe. Scared of him.

But not Miranda.

She was afraid, all right. But of herself, not him. She feared the bubbling inside her and the fact that she still wanted him despite last night and all that had happened.

Because of it.

Last night had been her first walk on the wild side, but not for lack of want. She'd spent her entire life suppressing the wildness, denying it. She'd unleashed it hoping to satisfy the craving, but it had backfired.

She wanted him even more now.

Only because she hadn't seen the monster fully unleashed. She'd had only a glimpse last night. Just enough to feed the stupid romantic fantasies that most women had when it came to vampires or pirates or rock stars.

But there was nothing romantic about the hunger. It was dark and twisted and consuming. Once she realized what he truly was, she would turn and run for her life.

"Has a man ever looked at you like this?" He swept a gaze over her, purposely drinking in the pout of her bottom lip, the fullness of her breasts beneath the T-shirt, her long, endless legs. Despite the oversized clothes, she still looked sexy as hell. Desire twisted inside of him and he felt his gaze darken, shift.

She drew a sharp breath. "Y-your eyes are purple." Her eyes widened. *"Purple."*

"Has a man ever touched you like this?" He didn't reach out. He didn't have to. His eyes did the reaching for him. His gaze dropped to the hem of her tank top and he concentrated. The cotton slid up inch by decadent inch until he saw a strip of bare stomach.

Surprise jerked through her and she glanced down just as the shirt paused above her belly button and the button on her shorts flicked open.

"No way," she breathed as the zipper slid open and the material started to shimmy down her hips.

She caught the edges and tried to yank them back up, but she was no match for his strength. The material kept moving until he could see the lacy vee of her panties and the sprinkle of blonde hair beneath.

"Has a man ever felt you like this?" He lifted his hand and made a motion with his fingers. A gasp bubbled from her lips. "You're warm."

"You're not touching me," she pointed out, shaking her head. "You're not really touching me." Disbelief glittered in her eyes along with something else.

Something dangerously close to desire.

The hunger twisted inside him and he barely resisted the sudden impulse to shove her up against the nearest wall, bury himself inside her delectable body and soak up her sweet, succulent energy. He needed it so bad.

He needed her.

He fought against the crazy notion. Any woman, he reminded himself. "If I'm not really touching you, then I'm sure you won't feel this." Another movement of his hand and shock gripped her.

Finally.

This was it. He'd finally gotten to her.

Her mouth opened and he waited for the piercing scream. The pure terror. The fear.

Instead, a gasp bubbled past her lips and her eyes clouded with passion.

He moved his fingers, intensifying the feelings, desperate to jolt some sense into her.

That this was real.

Frightening.

Fucking *scary*.

A moan curled up her throat. He could smell her essence growing stronger, more potent.

"I'm more than a man," he told her. And then he did what he should have done in the first place.

He stopped playing games and showed her the real Cody Braddock.

12

HE WAS A VAMPIRE.

The truth crystallized as Miranda found herself pinned against the second story of the house.

She glanced down to see that they were a good fifteen feet above the ground. His hard, muscular body pressed against her, holding her in place. But there was no one holding *him* in place. He stood suspended in midair. No wires or bungee cords.

His usually silver eyes glowed neon blue, as hot and bright as the center of a flame. His lips were pulled back, his fangs gleaming.

This was *not* happening.

She wasn't seeing this. Feeling this. Feeling *him*.

"You are." The deep timbre of his voice whispered through her head, but his lips didn't move. *"You can feel my heart beating in your chest, my blood pumping through your veins."*

The truth hit her as she became keenly aware of the double thump in her chest and the rhythm that echoed in her ears. Even more, she could feel the hunger that twisted inside of him, so demanding and fierce that it erased any lingering doubt.

A *vampire*.

The truth crystallized and slowly they drifted to the ground until she felt the solid earth beneath her feet.

"We're connected now," he added before he let her go. *"You drank from me and I drank from you."*

Her knees trembled and she braced one hand against the side of the house while the other went to her neck. She felt only smooth skin.

"Vampires don't just feed off of blood." He said the words out loud this time. "We also thirst for energy. Sexual energy. That's why I was in that club in the first place. I hadn't had sex in a couple of days and I was weak. I needed to build my strength up before I made the trip here."

"Why?" It was a tame question compared to the ones bombarding her senses, but it was all that popped out as she tried to fully comprehend what he was telling her.

"I'm here to kill the vampire who murdered my family."

"There's a vampire in Skull Creek?" The words came out in a high pitched squeak. *"Here?"*

"Actually, he's out of town for the next five days. But when he gets back, I'll be here. I've waited a long time for this. Too long."

Which meant he was sticking around until then.

The knowledge sent a zing of excitement through her, followed by a rush of *uh, oh*. One night, she reminded herself, despite the collage of images that rolled through her head.

The two of them naked on her front porch.

The two of them naked on the fifty-yard line.

The two of them *naked*.

"What else can you do?" she blurted, desperate to distract herself from the seductive scenario playing in her head. She glanced at the spot above where he'd had her pinned just seconds ago. "Besides levitating, that is."

"I can move things with my mind, but then you already know that." His words reminded her of the way he'd touched her, stroked her, stirred her without actually making physical contact. "I can also read thoughts and move really fast and hypnotize with my stare."

"Is that what you did to get me into that alley last night?"

His eyes, now molten silver, collided with hers. "I didn't have to do anything. You were more than willing on your own." His mouth drew into a tight line, as if he wasn't at all pleased about his next words. "You have a very lusty appetite."

The words echoed in her head and sparked a chain reaction of denial that gripped every muscle in her body. She'd fought too long and too hard to erase her past to have him make such an assumption. A completely false assumption. "Says you," she blurted. "You don't know me."

But that was the damned trouble of it all.

He did know her. He knew her fear. He felt it. It bubbled inside of her, making her lips tremble and her heart race.

Perfect, right?

He'd wanted to scare her. The problem was, she wasn't half afraid of him as she was of herself. Of the way he made her feel. Because even though she knew the truth—even though she'd seen it with her own eyes—she still wanted him. She couldn't forget last night. Or the way he'd made her feel.

He could feel it in the hard press of her nipples against his chest. He could smell the wet heat between her legs and see the frantic thump of her pulse. He could hear the desperate denial in her voice.

"For your information, I don't have one lusty bone in my body."

The urge to prove her wrong was fast and fierce, and Cody couldn't help himself. "You think?" Before she could reply, he captured her lips with his and kissed her with everything he had.

His tongue plunged deep and tangled with hers. He explored and tasted and stroked until her resistance fled. She relaxed against him. Her arms snaked around his neck and she held on tight. She kissed him back, meeting him stroke for stroke, pressing her body against his. Moving until his cock hardened and his hunger stirred.

His gut twisted and need roared inside of him. Stronger than anything he'd ever felt before.

Different.

Because *she* was different.

The thought struck and sent him whirling around, away from her.

Because that's what Cody Braddock did. He didn't stay too long or get too close. No ties. It was who he was now.

Who he'd always been.

HE *WAS* A VAMPIRE.

If there'd been any smidgeon of doubt, it disappeared

right along with Cody Braddock. Literally. One minute she stood facing him and the next, he was nowhere in sight. She was alone.

Thankfully.

The thought whispered through her head, reminding her of the wanton way she'd given in to his kiss and kissed him back just seconds ago.

Because he was a vampire.

Despite his denial about hypnotizing her, she knew he'd done *something*. That was the only explanation for the fierce desire that pushed and pulled inside of her and filled her with an urgency to do all sorts of shameful things.

She'd blamed last night's powerful reaction on the fact that he'd been the forbidden fruit—a cowboy—and she'd been as curious as Eve in the garden.

But if that had been the case, one bite would have satisfied her.

She wouldn't still want him.

More now than before.

Connected.

The word echoed in her head and she became acutely aware of the buzz of crickets. The sound seemed amplified, her hearing heightened just like her other senses. She could smell the fresh, sharp scent of newly turned earth. See the flutter of the June bugs that bounced off the security light near the corner of the house.

You drank from me and I drank from you.

She was hyped up on vamp blood. That explained the images. The feelings. Everything.

Not that it mattered.

Vampire or not, she wasn't going to hop into the back of a Chevy with him. Or do him on the front porch. Or the fifty-yard line. Or any of the other spots on her list. Even if he was sticking around for five days.

In fact, she was going to forget him and the list entirely. From this moment on, no thinking or fantasizing or *anything*.

At least that's what she told herself as she headed inside the house and pulled out the menu for next Saturday's Senior Sock Hop. She needed to do something normal. To finalize the details for the biggest social event at Golden Acres.

Hot dogs or hamburgers? Tapioca or banana?

She certainly didn't need to open up the Internet and spend three hours researching *vampires*.

The trouble was, she *wanted* to.

The feeling rose up inside her, consuming her thoughts to the point that she soon gave up the menu, killed the lights and headed upstairs.

Straight into an ice cold shower.

WAY TO GO, HOSS.

Cody damned himself as he punched the gas on his pick-up and hauled ass through town. His gut twisted and his insides ached. His fingers tightened on the steering wheel and he pushed the truck faster. There was no erasing her memory to weaken the link between them. Distance was all he had left.

That and the slim hope that another woman might be able to distract him.

He swung a sharp left and headed past the city limits.

A mile down, he saw the neon lights that spelled out The Iron Horse. A row of motorcycles sat out front, along with a few eighteen wheelers and a handful of pick-up trucks. For a Sunday night, the place was busy.

Then again, Skull Creek was little more than a map dot and chances were there weren't too many bars to choose from. It was also just a stone's throw from the main highway, which made for a crowded parking lot.

Cody turned into the gravel drive and pulled into a spot near the back. He pushed through the rear exit and stalled just inside the doorway. His gaze sliced through the smoky interior, scanning the various faces until he found what he was looking for.

She sat at one of the tables, her legs crossed, a cigarette dangling from one hand. She wore a pair of designer jeans and a simple button-up blouse that reminded him more of a soccer mom than a barfly.

As if she sensed his stare, her head snapped up and her gaze collided with his.

She was a soccer mom, all right, and she was fed up. Three ungrateful kids and an equally ungrateful husband had finally sent her over the edge. She'd packed up her car and was headed to her sister's house over in Houston. The minute she hit town, she was filing for divorce and granting him full custody of the kids.

The truth left a bad taste in his mouth and he glanced around. But the only other women were locals. He was going to be sticking around town for the next few days. He could make her forget, but he'd just found out the hard way that even that wasn't foolproof.

The last thing he needed was a lovesick woman hanging around his motel room, drawing attention to his presence. He shifted his focus back to the soccer mom. A stranger just passing through was exactly what he needed. No awkward morning after. No expectations.

Just sex. Sweet, rejuvenating sex.

He started for her table.

"Is this seat taken?" he asked when he reached her.

She hesitated. As determined as she was, she'd never actually done anything like this. At the same time, if she was serious about ditching her relationship with John— and she was—there was no better time to start than the present. She'd given him fifteen years of her life. She'd cooked and cleaned and ironed his stupid shirts. She'd endured not one but three C-sections and raised a trio of hateful, selfish boys that were just like their father. She'd even cooked the Christmas turkey every year so that John's mother wouldn't have to go to any trouble, and all so he could take his big boobed assistant to Hawaii instead of his devoted wife. Like hell. She deserved her own reward for all those years of hard labor. She deserved this.

She took a long swallow of her wine and motioned to the chair. "Help yourself. So," she sipped more wine as he settled in. "Are you from around here?"

"Just passing through."

"Me, too." Her gaze caught and held his. "You know, you look familiar. You don't have friends in San Antonio, do you? That's where I'm from. Maybe I've seen you before—"

"No," he cut in. "No friends in San Antonio." He let

his gaze slide over her, noting her short red hair and fair skin. She had a small chest and a narrow waist. No long blonde hair or lush curves. Nothing like Miranda.

And this was bad?

It wasn't. It was damned good. He needed to forget her. And last night. And the damned way she'd welcomed him into her hot, lush body. And the fact that she was thinking about him at that very moment. Wanting him.

"So how about going back to my place?" he asked, determined to get on with things before he changed his mind.

Not that he would. Hell, no. He was hungry. That was all. Hunger made for impatience. No use beating around the bush.

She held up her glass. "Aren't you even going to offer me a drink first?"

"Is that what you really want?"

I'd rather have you. That's what her body said. She was on fire, desperate for someone to hold her, appreciate her, need her the way her husband never had.

But her head… Her head wasn't so sure she wanted to go through with this. She'd never done anything like this. Ever.

Cody caught and held her gaze for a brief moment and her doubt fled.

"Let's go," she murmured, pushing to her feet. She took his hand and led him out to the parking lot. "We can take my car." She hit the lock fob and the lights flashed on a black Beemer just a few feet away.

Cody was just reaching for the doorknob when he felt the rippling awareness. He turned and came face-to-face with the one person he'd been desperately trying to outrun for the past few years.

"I thought that was you." Benny James smiled and Cody couldn't shake the sudden feeling that he was totally screwed.

13

EASY.

The word echoed through Cody's head as he faced off with the pain-in-the-ass reporter who'd been dogging him for the past several months.

Benny wore a pair of faded jeans and a green T-shirt that read The Truth Shall Set You Free. Not that he was the religious sort. It was the name of a band he'd played in back in college. Cody knew that much from the numerous run-ins he'd already had with the man.

Right now, however, he could read nothing in the man's gaze because it was hidden beneath a pair of Costa Del Mars.

"Isn't it a little dark out for glasses?" Cody arched an eyebrow.

"I've got sensitive eyes."

That, or he'd finally figured out the truth.

The possibility sent a rush of alarm through Cody. His hands tightened and his muscles went tense.

"The minute I spotted you inside," Benny went on, "I said to myself, that's got to be Cody Boyd. But then my sanity kicked in and I realized that it couldn't be Cody Boyd because Cody Boyd is supposed to be headed for Vegas right now. At least that's what his publicist told me this morning when I called her." His mouth drew into a tight line. "But you aren't headed for Vegas, are you? You're right here in Skull Creek." A click echoed in Cody's ears and he knew James had hit the record button on the small unit in his pocket. "I'm sure the fans would love to know what you're doing here. Besides picking up women, that is."

Cody shrugged. "She's just giving me a lift. What about you? What are you doing here?"

"I go where the stories go. You're on fire right now, thanks to that last ride. Everybody who follows the bull riding circuit wants to hear your plans for after the win in Vegas. Provided you do actually win."

"I'll win," Cody said.

James shrugged. "So what's up next for the infamous Cody Boyd? Retirement?"

"Maybe."

"Come on. You've been on the circuit for fifteen years now. You've got to be well into your thirties." When Cody gave him a sharp glance, he added, "Not that you look it, buddy. You don't look a day over twenty-five. Speaking of which, I'm sure the fans would like to hear how you keep such a youthful appearance in such a grueling sport. Diet? Exercise? Botox?"

"I only eat organic. Listen, I'm in a hurry. I've got an early day tomorrow."

"But I haven't gotten to the juicy questions yet—"

"Call my publicist. She can issue an FAQ sheet. I'm late."

"For what?" James shoved the handheld recorder in Cody's face. "A little R & R with your friend, there?"

"I'm catching a red-eye flight for Vegas to do some preliminary PR stuff before the PBR finals." Cody pushed the microphone aside and climbed into the car. Keying the engine, he gunned it and left Benny staring after him.

Shit.

Shit. Shit. *Shit.*

The last thing he needed was James dogging him, asking questions, *watching.*

He'd seen the man jot down the BMW plates. He had no doubt he would be looking up the woman in the passenger's seat to get the scoop on her night with the infamous Cody Boyd.

Not that she was going to have anything to tell him.

Time to bail.

"What was that stuff about Vegas—" his companion started, her words dying a quick death when he caught her gaze and held it. Her stare went blank and he shifted his attention back to the road. He hit the interstate and drove for the next fifteen minutes before he found a Motel 6 and pulled into the parking lot.

Soccer mom stared through the glass and blinked several times as reality seemed to settle in. She turned toward him. "I thought you were taking me home with you? Not that I mind a motel. It'll do just as well—"

"Not tonight."

"But—"

"It's okay," he cut in, staring deep into her eyes. Her gaze sparked and then it was as if a candle flame had been blown out.

"You're okay," he told her. "You stopped for a drink

while waiting for your car. Had a few too many and the bartender dropped you off here. Now you're going to go inside, register for a room and sleep off the alcohol. You'll forget everything and everyone you've seen in the past half hour. In the morning, you get back on the road for Houston. Understood?"

She nodded, her eyes vacant and empty.

"And one more thing. Lose the husband if you have to, but not the kids. They need you. Even if they don't know it."

Once she climbed from the cab and disappeared into the motel lobby, Cody shoved the truck into reverse and pulled out of the parking lot. Hanging a left back on the interstate, he headed for Skull Creek and his own motel room.

As much as he wanted to, he couldn't afford to feed right now. Not with James *this* close.

No way had Cody ditched the soccer mom because he didn't *want* to have sex with her. *Hell,* no. He was a vampire, for Christ's sake. He wanted every woman. Even if she didn't have long blonde hair and lush curves and the most incredible whiskey-colored eyes.

Every woman.

But not with James watching him.

Tomorrow he would call his publicist and have her drop a hint that Cody had stopped off in Skull Creek to order a custom chopper before heading for Vegas. James would buy it and get off his back. Cody could then get back to the business at hand—forgetting Miranda and building up his strength for the coming showdown with Garret Sawyer.

Cody intended to win.

He would make Sawyer pay once and for all and maybe, just maybe, he would finally have some peace.

IF SHE SAW ANOTHER VAMPIRE blog, she was going to slit her wrists.

Who knew there were so many?

Most were normal humans with a vampire fetish, but there were a few posts here and there that rang true.

Because vampires really and truly existed and she just so happened to have the hots for one.

She didn't want to have the hots for Cody. She wanted to forget. To throw herself into planning the following week's activities for the senior center. Monday morning would come early and she had to have everyone divided up into Bunko teams.

Not that everyone would want to play.

Mr. Sherman would claim he couldn't sit still because of his recent hernia operation. Maureen Westerlee would gripe that she couldn't do anything that would distract her from the Wife Swap re-runs on Lifetime. Sue Lynn Crapple would swear Bunko was too much like Bingo and she hated Bingo. But Miranda had to do the team assignments anyway on the off chance that everyone would want to join in.

She didn't need to waste her Sunday evening fantasizing about Cody. Or the list. Or Cody and the list.

He's a bloodsucking vampire. Dangerous. Deadly.

That's what she told herself.

If only she believed it.

But he'd saved her last night and he'd even driven her

home. He wasn't going to hurt her. Not physically, anyway.

Not emotionally either, she reminded herself. Because it was over. She'd had her orgasm and now it was time to get on with her life.

That's what she told herself as she pulled on an oversized T-shirt and climbed into bed. She was going to forget Cody and the all-important fact that he was hanging around town for the next few days. Instead, she was going to focus on her job and her future and sleep.

She definitely needed sleep.

When she closed her eyes, however, she didn't drift off. Instead, she thought about him. And the way he'd touched her in the alley behind the club. And the way he'd kissed her in the backyard.

And how much *she* wanted to kiss *him*.

Because of him.

He'd worked his magic on her. Entranced her. Now she was hooked and there was no way she *couldn't* think about him and the fact that he was right here in town. Close.

Waiting.

To give her another orgasm.

Nine of them to be exact.

The moment the thought struck, she tried to push it back out. She didn't want to think about the damned list. Or what it would be like to visit each spot with Cody Braddock. At the same time, she couldn't *not* think about it. He was in her head. Under her skin. There was no escaping the lust.

She had to deal with it. To burn a little off and then

maybe, just maybe, she could satisfy her curiosity and get him out of her system.

And if not?

It didn't matter, because Cody would be gone. He was only here for five days. Then it was out of sight, out of mind. Right?

She could only hope. She climbed out of bed and headed for her closet. Pulling on a pair of shorts, she knotted her T-shirt at her waist and reached for the pink boots she'd worn last night. She slid her feet into them and drew a deep breath.

And then she headed out to make vampire Cody a proposition he couldn't refuse.

14

SHE WANTED SEX.

Cody knew it the moment he opened his hotel room door and found Miranda standing on his doorstep.

It was a truth that had nothing to do with the fact that he could read every lustful thought racing through her brain.

Rather, he saw it in the trembling of her full lips, the high color in her cheeks, the tense set to her shoulders, the outline of her ripe nipples against the T-shirt that she wore. It was much more snug than the oversized number she'd had on earlier and it emphasized the full shape of her breasts and narrow tuck of her waist. Her shorts revealed long, shapely legs accented by the pink cowboy boots she'd had on last night.

His groin tightened and his erection stirred.

Her scent—warm, sweet apples and decadent woman—teased his nostrils. Her soft breaths echoed in his ears.

She licked her full lips and he felt the moist stroke on the head of his dick. "I need to talk to you." Another swipe of her tongue on her trembling bottom lip and she added, "I've got a proposition for you."

She rubbed her lips together and he almost groaned out

loud. "You feed off sex, right?" Before he could answer, she rushed on, "Which means you *need* to have sex like I need a really good pizza every Friday night. Right?"

"I've never heard it compared to a double pepperoni with extra cheese, but yeah. Something like that. And this matters because?"

"I need sex, too. I mean, I don't *need* it. I want it." Her gaze met his and he saw the seductive thoughts that haunted her. "I can't stop thinking about last night. About us. About you." *Because of you.*

That's what she wanted to think. What she'd convinced herself of and while Cody knew it wasn't the least bit true, he wasn't going to point it out to her and put her on the defensive.

She was here and he wanted her to stay.

The hunger, he reminded himself. He hadn't fed and so he wasn't thinking clearly.

It wasn't *her*. Or the softness in her whiskey-colored eyes when she looked at him or the warmth of her body so close to his own. And it sure as hell wasn't the methodical sound of her breaths that echoed in his head. Or the steady beat of her heart that sped up every time her gaze collided with his. Or the simple knowledge that someone was there and for the first time in his afterlife he didn't feel so painfully alone.

The thought struck and he stiffened. Since when did he give a rat's ass about being alone? He liked it. No one to worry over. To disappoint. It's who he was. Who he would always be.

"You want to have sex with me," he stated, suddenly desperate to hurry the encounter along. She would proposition him. He would say no. The end. "That's it, right? That's why you're here?"

"Not just any old sex. I want to have sex behind the bleachers at the football stadium. The gazebo in the town square. The history section of the library. The feed store. And a few others. See, there's this list—"

"Restroom Randy's Hottest Sex Spots," he cut in. "I know."

"But how—" she started, the words stalling as she shook her head. "Duh. You're a vampire. You know everything about me."

"I know what you're thinking at the moment you're thinking it. But only if I stare into your eyes."

"So if I turn around?" She put her back to him. "You can't read my mind?"

"I can feel what you feel, but I can't pick your brain."

"That's a relief."

"And why is that?"

"It's not fair that it should be so one-sided. No one should know everything in a relationship. But then this isn't an actual relationship. It's business." She turned back around. "If you agree to have sex with me in every spot on the list, that is."

Yes. The answer raged through him, but he clamped his lips shut. *You're already in too deep, buddy. Don't make things worse.* "So who came up with this list?" he asked instead.

She shrugged. "Just this guy I used to know. He thought up this brilliant idea to write down the ten hottest places where he and I supposedly did it."

"Supposedly?"

"We didn't actually do anything. We went out once and he tried to feel me up. I turned him down. He got pissed off and made up the list."

"And people believed him?"

"My name was Rivers, so it had to be true."

Because she came from a long line of women who had no qualms about stripping bare and getting it on in the middle of a football stadium, or any of the other nine spots.

"So? Are you interested or not?"

"Maybe."

"Meaning?"

"First I want to know why you're doing this."

"You're the one with super vampire senses. Don't you already know?"

"Yes, but I want to see if you do." He stared deep into her gaze and saw the desperation. Despite her words, she didn't just want this. She needed it. To satisfy the wildness inside her. To calm the restlessness. To distract herself from the fact that she wasn't nearly as satisfied with her life as she pretended to be. "You won't ever get enough," he pointed out, his voice deep and knowing. "Doing it once. Twice. Three times. You'll just want more."

"Says you. You're a vampire who feeds off sex. It's different for me. I've spent too much time trying not to think about sex, really great, exciting, fulfilling sex. It only stands to reason that's all I can think about now. I need to sow a few wild oats. Cut loose. Enjoy the moment. Then my curiosity will be satisfied."

Even more, you'll be gone. No temptation. No fall from grace.

Or so she desperately hoped.

"So will you do it?" she added. "Eight encounters. Eight different places."

"If there are ten spots, then why just eight encounters?"

"We already did the back alley. Granted, it was outside of a bar rather than a Piggly Wiggly, but an alley's an alley."

"And number ten?"

Her eyes clouded and she stiffened. "I'm not interested in that one. If you've seen one backseat, you've seen them all. It's just the other eight. You help me fulfill those and you'll get to feed. I'll keep my mouth shut about your identity and you won't have to worry about pissing off the angry villagers."

"And if I don't?"

"We've never had a vampire in town before. I'm sure the newspaper will put you on the front page when I go to them with your story."

If they believed her, which she really didn't think they would. But she was using it to bargain anyway because she wanted this.

She wanted him.

"So what about it? Are you in?"

It was the last thing he needed to agree to. He wouldn't just be going back for seconds, he'd be going back for thirds and fourths and so on. Letting her under his skin. Into his thoughts. Fortifying the connection.

At the same time, he had five entire days until Garret Sawyer flew back into town. Five days to feed and build his strength, and Miranda was offering him the perfect sustenance.

And a prime opportunity no sane vampire in his situation could resist.

Feeding off of several different women with Benny James so close on his tail wasn't the smartest thing to do. The last thing he needed was to stir Benny's curiosity even more by cruising the local bars and picking up females.

If he said yes to Miranda, he could maintain his low profile and stay off of Benny's radar.

It made sense despite the alarm bells ringing in his head. *No ties,* a voice screamed. *No friggin' ties!*

"Okay."

"Great," she blurted as if he'd just agreed to cut her lawn. "We can start first thing in the morning."

"Why not right now? We've got eight encounters and only five days. It seems a shame to waste time."

She glanced at her watch. "It's already midnight. I have to work tomorrow. We're starting a breakfast bunko tournament and I have to be there early. Not to mention, I'm smack dab in the middle of deciding on appetizers for the food buffet at next week's senior sock hop. I'm the activities coordinator at Golden Acres. It's a nursing/retirement village just outside of town."

"Breakfast Bunko?"

"I know it doesn't sound all that fun, but the residents play for cinnamon rolls and it's really a blast. Especially if Erwin Holiday wins. He's allergic to cinnamon and so he raffles off his winnings to the highest bidder. It just prolongs the fun that much more."

"I'll bet."

"It's settled then. We'll start tomorrow." Namely

because as eager as she was, she was also scared. Scared to give in to the wildness inside of her. Scared to stop planning and simply act. Scared to lose her precious control.

"I thought you wanted to cut loose? Enjoy the moment?" His gaze collided with hers and called to the wildness inside of her. "The moment is now, not later, sugar."

She wanted to say yes. She wanted it so badly that her entire body trembled. A reaction that both scared and excited her, and Cody couldn't wait to see which emotion would win out.

She licked her lips and he stiffened. His groin tightened and he shifted his stance. Her attention dropped to the very prominent erection pushing against his jeans and she swallowed.

"Okay," she finally murmured. "Let's do it."

"Atta girl." He grinned.

And then he swooped her up into his arms and headed for the nearest feed store.

15

MIRANDA STARED UP AT THE John Deere 400 front loader and wondered what sort of drugs Ray McGuire had been smoking when he'd added *this* to the *Hottest Sex Spots* list.

While the huge green scoop bucket attached to the nose could easily hold two people, it didn't look even remotely comfortable, much less a prime rendezvous spot.

Ditto for the other pieces of farm equipment that crowded the back lot of Jimbo's Feed and Farm. The gigantic red metal building perched on the far edge of town, along with a handful of other businesses, all of which had closed up shop much earlier that evening. There was Skull Creek Stables, a boarding facility for cattle and horses, The Handy Dandy Lumber yard, Jimbo's Feed & Farm Equipment and the Happy Tails Pet Resort. A few acres separated each establishment, affording plenty of privacy for tonight's rendezvous.

Sort of.

A twelve-foot chain link fence enclosed the back lot behind Jimbo's where the machinery was kept. Beyond the fence, pastureland reached toward a distant patch of trees. Several horses being boarded at the stables grazed in the far distance, instantly alert to the man who stood behind her. They stomped and whinnied in response to the danger lurking close by.

Miranda didn't blame them.

Not that Cody would ever hurt a defenseless animal. Vampire or not, he wouldn't. She wasn't sure how she knew, except that she did. It was a certainty that sat deep inside, along with the knowledge that she wanted him. That she couldn't help but want him.

Raw power radiated from his body. A fierce magnetism that made her want to turn and throw herself into his arms even though her precious list mentioned nothing about getting it on next to a chain link fence.

Desire welled inside her and made her hands tremble. She drew a deep, shaky breath and fought for control as his smooth, deep voice slid into her ears.

"I can see the appeal."

"Are you kidding me?" She focused her attention on the front loader and tried to ignore the fact that his chest kissed her shoulder blades. He was so close.

Not close enough.

"That thing will barely fit two people," she blurted, eager to distract herself from the wanton thought. "There's no room to move."

"There's always the tractor seat."

"It's one seat."

"That's the point, sugar." His lips fanned the outer shell of one ear and her stomach hollowed out.

Anticipation ripped through her, so strong and fierce that her reservations kicked in and she blurted, "It doesn't matter anyway because there's no way we're getting in there. The gate is locked. I told you we should wait until tomorrow—" The words stumbled into a loud squeal as he scooped her into his arms.

Effortlessly, they sailed up and over the barrier. A heartbeat later, he set her on her feet next to the John Deere. Her body did a slow glide down his and her heart stopped when she felt his arousal against her belly. He was thick and hard and the temperature outside seemed to kick up at least ten degrees.

"Superheroes aren't the only ones who can leap fences in a single bound," he murmured, his voice gruff. Sexy.

She swallowed. "That would be *tall buildings*." She licked her suddenly dry lips.

"I can do those, too." A grin tugged at his sensuous mouth and then, just like that, he disappeared.

She blinked, staring at the empty spot in front of her.

"Up here." His deep voice drew her attention and she glanced up to see him standing in front of the tractor seat. The moonlight outlined his tall, powerful frame and made him seem almost surreal. His gaze brightened, the edges turning a bright, brilliant purple as he reached down a hand. "Your turn."

She stared at his long powerful fingers and a very real image rushed at her—her body straddling his, his mouth suckling her nipple, his strong hands playing up and down her spine. Heat zapped her and the air stalled in her lungs. She hesitated.

A startling reaction considering the fact that he was calling the shots, bending her to his will, filling her with an uncontrollable lust.

He was the reason she was obsessed with the list.

He'd walked into her life and bam, all she could think about was the two of them getting it on at each and every sex spot. Only when he waltzed out of her life and took his vampire mojo with him would she stop walking around like some sex-starved zombie.

He was the one making her feel so wild and reckless and desperate.

It certainly had nothing to do with her legacy or the fact that she might be more like her mother and sisters than she wanted to believe.

Him.

Holding tight to the thought, she slid her hand into his and let him pull her up onto the riding deck.

He turned her so that her back was to him and then he sat down. Pulling her after him, he settled her onto his lap, his crotch nestled against her buttocks.

He was rock hard.

The realization sent a rush of electricity to every major hot spot—her nipples, her belly button, the tender insides of her thighs, the backs of her knees, the tips of her toes. Her body tingled and a wave of heat swept through her.

Cody slid his arms around her waist and cupped the undersides of her breasts, and her heart stopped completely.

Miranda stiffened against the warmth that unfurled inside of her and swept across her nerve endings. She opened her mouth and drew a steady breath.

The air lodged in her lungs when he swept a hand down and touched the vee between her legs. She felt the pressure of his touch through the denim of her shorts and electricity skimmed up and down her spine. He rasped her, back and forth, making her head spin and her lungs fight for air. The sensation was overwhelming. At the same time, it wasn't enough. She wanted more.

A surge of longing welled inside and she had the sudden urge to stand up and strip off every piece of clothing. She wanted him to see her naked. She wanted to see him naked.

She wanted it really, *really* bad.

Too bad for a woman who'd prided herself on *not* being a slave to her lust. Her head ruled. Nothing else. Even in this situation.

Especially in this situation.

She braced her hands on his thighs and dug her fingers into the hard, corded muscles and held on tight to what little self-control remained. She might be powerless, but she wasn't losing herself completely.

Not for Cody Braddock.

Not for anyone.

Man or vampire.

SHE WANTED TO MOVE.

Cody wasn't staring into her eyes, but he knew it anyway. He could feel the need vibrating inside of her, hear the frantic thud of her pulse and smell the heady, sweet scent of her excitement.

He slid her zipper down and dipped a fingertip into her panties, between her legs. When his fingertip made direct contact with her clit, she gasped. A violent tremor shook her body. Her breasts trembled. Her shoulders quaked. But she didn't turn and press herself against him. She wouldn't. No matter how much she wanted to.

Because she wanted to.

Need twisted at his gut and his own hunger stirred. He stood them both up then and stripped her bare. Her shorts hit the ground first, followed by her panties. Her T-shirt. Her bra. Then he turned his attention to his own clothes. He tossed his shirt and peeled off his jeans and underwear.

When they were both naked, he settled back down onto the seat and turned her. Catching one leg, he urged her to straddle him.

Her wet heat surrounded his cock in one downward glide that robbed him of his thoughts and stirred a ferocious growl. He stiffened, his hands holding her tight for a long moment as he relished the incredible warmth.

The sensation took her breath away, as well, and melted the resistance inside of her. She grasped his shoulders and braced herself as she finally succumbed to the desire swamping her. She rotated her hips, her inner muscles contracting, sucking at him, teasing the beast, stirring the hunger.

He grasped her buttocks, his fingers sinking into her flesh, soaking in her sweet heat. Her eyes were closed, her head tilted back as she rode him. A fine sheen of perspiration covered her skin. Her breasts bobbed, her nipples hard and rosy and so damned mouthwatering.

She was the most beautiful woman he'd ever seen.

And for a brief, crazy moment, he had the distinct feeling that he would never meet another like her. No one as beautiful. As wild. As different.

She was it. She was *his*.

He shook away the notion and focused on the clenching in his gut. He tightened his pelvis and thrust upward at the same time that she pushed down. He went deeper only to urge her back up and thrust again. And again.

Miranda caught her bottom lip against the sensation spiraling through her. The pressure built, getting sharper and sweeter until she couldn't take anymore. Heat exploded, rushing through her body at an alarming pace that sucked the oxygen from her chest and made her head spin. Her muscles clenched. Her nerves vibrated. Her brain buzzed.

"Look at me." The command whispered through her head and despite the fireworks going off, she forced her eyes open in time to see Cody's eyes fire-blue then purple. His nostrils flared. A hiss worked its way up his throat. His lips drew back and his fangs glittered and she could feel the hunger pushing and pulling inside of him.

It tore at him, demanding sustenance despite the fact that he was already feeding off her climax. She felt it in the draw of his hands where he touched her, the pull of his erection still full and throbbing inside her.

She knew what he needed and staring deep into his eyes, she couldn't deny him. No woman could. He was a vampire weaving his magic, mesmerizing her with a glance.

A vampire. That explained the way she rode him with such abandon. The way her skin flushed hot when he looked at her and her knees went weak at his touch. It explained the way she became acutely aware of the pulse at her neck that seemed to keep time with the throbbing between her legs.

It was him.

His charm.

His magic.

His desperation.

She felt it as intensely as she felt her own climax and she couldn't help but try to ease his pain.

She slid her hands around his neck and drew him to her. Her head fell back and she closed her eyes as she guided his lips to her pulse beat.

16

CODY FELT THE INTOXICATING throb against his tongue and heat exploded in his belly. His jaw ached and his fangs tingled. The very tip of his incisor rasped her tender flesh and desire speared him. One sweet drop of blood beaded on her fragrant skin, the scent teasing and tempting.

The salty sweet taste hit his tongue and sent a firebomb straight down his throat to his stomach. Heat exploded and his body shook and it was all he could do to force himself away.

But he did.

He slid his lips down, licking at her throat, nibbling her collarbone. But not drinking.

Drinking from her as she'd drank from him would solidify the connection between them. Distance wouldn't matter then. There would be no pushing her out of his thoughts. His heart.

He shook off the last notion and concentrated on holding tight to his control. He might have agreed to the sex. But he wouldn't—*couldn't*—indulge in her blood.

Her body, however, was a different story.

He'd been there, done that, and so the damage was already done. No sense denying himself.

He tightened his grip on her bottom, anchoring her in place as he thrust upward. Her insides tightened around him, milking him and the sensation sent him over the edge. His climax hit him hard and fast, like the swift jerk of an angry bull. He stiffened, hanging on for dear life as the adrenaline rushed through him and every nerve in his body started to vibrate.

Cody slid his arms around her and held her tight. Relishing the frantic beat of her heart against his chest. Feeling it inside his own.

Not that it felt half as good as his eight seconds, he reminded himself.

Hell, no. That high was much more potent and satisfying.

This… This was just sex.

Sustenance.

The end.

The two words echoed, so clear and distinct, in Miranda's head and she stiffened.

"It's not like I think there's more to this than there is," she said as she climbed off of him. "Trust me, I know it's just sex, and I know it doesn't mean anything."

His gaze narrowed. "I thought you weren't the meaningless sex type?"

"I'm not." *Regardless of what the folks in town might think.*

The minute the thought echoed in her head, his gaze narrowed and she knew he'd picked up every word. "It doesn't matter what other people think." His voice was deep and gruff. "All that matters is what you think."

"Easy for you to say. You don't live here." Grabbing

the steering wheel, she held on as she climbed down to the ground and retrieved her panties. Her skin heated as she slid them on, all the while conscious of his gaze.

"If it bothers you, pick up and move."

"Believe me, I've thought about it."

"But?"

"But this is home." She shrugged and snatched up her T-shirt. "The only one I've ever had." She slid the soft cotton over her head and tried to ignore the fact that he was still perched in the tractor seat, still naked. "Besides, things have changed some. Once people realized I wasn't the same as my mother and sisters, they started treating me differently. There are still quite a few who haven't come around, but I can't say as I really blame them. My mother wasn't the most upstanding woman."

"Too much meaningless sex?"

"Exactly. The thing was," she blurted, desperate to distract herself from the nearly overwhelming urge to ditch the panties and climb back into his lap for another ride, "she wasn't after meaningless sex. She thought it meant something." She grabbed her shorts. "Unfortunately none of the men she brought home ever did." She stuffed her legs into the denim and pulled them up. "They were just using her and she let them."

"The way you're letting me use you?" The voice came from directly behind her and she turned to find him fully clothed, his shirt buttoned as if he hadn't just been buck naked in the seat of a John Deere.

"This is different. I don't have a choice."

She *didn't*, she reminded herself. *Vampire. Mind*

control. She didn't stand a chance. Sure, she'd been the one to proposition him. But only because he'd manipulated her to the point that she couldn't stop thinking about him. And the list. And sex. Miranda had no choice in the situation.

Her mother had had a choice. She'd had the power to say no and walk away from the endless string of cowboys who'd propositioned her. Instead, she'd given up her power for pleasure. And when that pleasure had turned into the pain of rejection, she'd given up her life.

Her daughters.

"It doesn't mean she didn't love you." His deep voice slid into her ears and eased the vise tightening in her chest. "She did. She just didn't know how to show it because she was too busy trying to deal with whatever was eating her up inside. Loneliness, maybe. Insecurity."

"How would you know?"

He shrugged. "Because I've been there." His gaze met hers. "Sometimes people get so busy running from their own demons that they can't stop long enough to see what matters most. Not until it's too late."

What happened?

It was there on the tip of her tongue, but she held it back. The less she knew about Cody Braddock, the better. Even if she was extremely curious. About the man he'd once been. The vampire he'd become. The vampire he pursued. Her gaze went to the small scar on his face and the questions burned inside of her.

She stiffened. "It's getting late. We really ought to get out of here."

He looked as if he wanted to say something, but then

he swept her off her feet. In the blink of an eye, they stood on the opposite side of the fence.

"Tomorrow night," she blurted as he set her on her feet. "The football stadium. Nine o'clock." And then Miranda turned and walked away from Cody Braddock.

Because she *wasn't* her mother.

While she might not be able to resist Cody physically, she could damned well resist him emotionally. That meant keeping her real life and her fantasies separate. No talking to Cody, getting to know him. No sharing the past or the present or the future with him. No getting hung up on him, *consumed* by him the way her mother had done time and time again with every man in her past. Nothing.

Just sex.

CODY WATCHED HER WALK AWAY and damned himself for wanting to go after her. For once, he wasn't going to let his common sense take a backseat to impulse.

He fought the urge and focused on the tingling in his body.

It was the sex.

He could still feel the rush of warmth, the zing of electricity as the current flowed into him and he soaked up her delicious energy. Even more damning was the sizzle of excitement and the rush of pleasure as he'd exploded inside of her.

Again.

He'd written off the first orgasm as a fluke. But tonight… He'd crashed and burned so quickly that it bothered him.

She bothered him because she was different from all

the women in his past. They'd all done their damnedest to be as sexy, as alluring as possible. But Miranda did her damnedest NOT to be. She was holding back.

He'd felt it in the trembling of her body. The stiffness as she'd tried to resist the impulses pushing and pulling inside of her.

Despite her determination to cut loose and live out the damned list, she wasn't letting go completely. She was afraid to go with her feelings, to follow her lust, to let it rule her. Afraid she might like it too much.

She would never admit such a thing. She'd convinced herself it was *his* fault. The uncontrollable lust. The need. The urgency.

She was wrong. While he was completely capable of mesmerizing her, he hadn't done any such thing. She was reacting to him because of her own desire.

Even now, as she walked the short distance back to the motel to pick up her car, she was still burning for him, her nipples pebbled, her sex moist. He could see her in his mind's eye, feel her heartbeat in his chest.

And she could feel him.

He slid the button in place on his jeans and his fingertips grazed the head of his cock. Her soft sigh echoed in his head as her breath caught. She'd felt it, too.

Just to prove it, he stroked himself. Once. Twice. He heard her sharp intake of breath. Felt the trembling in her fingers. Smelled the wet heat between her legs.

She felt him, all right, on a level that went much deeper than anything he'd ever experienced. And damned if he didn't like it.

He'd spent his entire afterlife tuning into everyone

else with his heightened senses, but no one had ever tuned in to him.

Until now.

Miranda had drank from him and in doing so, she'd taken in a piece of him. He was a part of her.

His mind did a fast rewind to their encounter and he saw her sitting on his lap, her head tilted and her back arched as she offered herself to him.

She'd felt his hunger, and she'd understood.

His mother had been the only other female to ever really get what lurked inside of him as a man. The restlessness. The desperation. The fear. And so she'd let him do as he pleased, making excuses for him, putting up with him. She'd known he needed to burn off the steam before it burned him up from the inside out.

Once he'd turned into a vampire, the restlessness had turned to something much darker and more consuming. Something far more powerful than anyone could conceive. But Miranda had understood. He hadn't coaxed or mesmerized or enticed her.

She'd accepted who he was, what he was, and offered herself of her own volition.

The realization shook him to the core and conjured all sorts of crazy thoughts. Like maybe, just maybe, Miranda Rivers wasn't just the only woman to give him an orgasm. Maybe she was the only woman, period.

The woman.

So? While she might be *the* woman, no way was he *the* man. He was a vampire, for Christ's sake. Even more, he was wild. Reckless. The exact opposite of the nice, reliable, safe type she envisioned for her future.

The truth bothered him a hell of a lot more than it should have and sent Cody over the fence toward the handful of horses that grazed in the adjacent pasture.

They spooked immediately, but he was too fast for them. In a flash, he gripped the mane of one of the cutting horses and hauled himself onto her back. The animal's survival instincts kicked in and she went crazy, twisting and bucking while Cody held on tight.

The ride got wilder and more intense, the animal desperate to get loose of the demon clinging to her. But Cody wouldn't let go.

His fingers clenched and his thigh muscles tensed. He arched his back and leaned into the movement. Adrenaline pumped through him. His nerves trembled. His brain buzzed. The horse twisted, his muscles jerked, and his entire body came alive.

It was a feeling he knew all too well.

One that didn't begin to compare with what he'd felt when he'd exploded inside of Miranda.

Bullshit!

He was riding a goddamned *cutting horse*. Of course the ride wasn't as fierce. If he'd been on the back of an ornery bull, that would have been different. More intense. More explosive. Much more than any orgasm.

All the more reason to deal with Garret Sawyer as soon as possible and get the hell out of here. Back to his career. He was at the top of his game. Living for the moment. Enjoying it.

Miranda might be denying her wild side, but Cody liked his. It was the one thing that kept him going day after day, year after year. The one thing that made an eternity bearable.

The thought of settling down in one place, of denying his impulsive side for the rest of his existence made him want to stake himself.

Walk away.

That's what he'd always done in the past. What Miranda fully expected him to do once his business in Skull Creek was finished.

Cody had no intention of disappointing her.

He just wished that fact didn't suddenly bother him so damned much.

17

"I'LL SEE THEM FANCY LACE britches and raise you one Double D Playtex Extra Support with removable inserts." The declaration came from Eula Holly, a small, stick-like woman in her nineties. She had dyed red hair and a pair of matching eyebrows that she'd had tattooed on during a shopping trip to Austin last year. She pursed her pink frosted lips and reached for the edge of her flower-print blouse.

"Hold it," said the old woman to her right.

Beula was Eula's twin sister. Same pink frosted lipstick. Same dyed hair. Beula had opted not to go for the eyebrow tattoos, however. She'd gotten her belly button pierced instead.

Needless to say, Miranda had made a promise to never leave either of them alone with a debit card ever again.

"Don't you dare let the girls loose," Beula told her twin. "How many times do I have to tell you? This ain't strip poker. It's bunko. B-U-N-K-O."

"Bunko?" Eula adjusted the thick bifocals that sat on her pointy nose and looked around as if seeing everything for the first time. "If this ain't strip poker, then why is there a pair of underpants sitting front and center?"

"That's not undies. It's a doily."

"A dolly?" Eula adjusted the glasses again and leaned closer to look at the center of the table. "That don't look like no dolly to me."

"Not a do—llee. A doyyy-leee. You know, for stuff to sit on. Martha Hamburg crocheted it especially for our table. See?" Beula pointed a bony finger. "It's got our team name—The Bunko Bimbos—right there in pink thread."

Eula leaned even closer and reality seemed to strike. "Why, it certainly does." She smiled. "That's some nice craftsmanship."

"Glad you approve. Now can you hurry it up and roll?" Beula shoved the dice into her sister's gnarled hand. "I'd like to get a turn before my arteries harden."

Eula started shaking the dice while Beula chanted, "Come on, twenty-one!"

Miranda glanced at the plate full of cinnamon rolls sitting near Beula before moving on to make sure that the next table had plenty of "stakes" to play with.

She'd started Breakfast Bunko when she'd first come on board as the activities coordinator at Golden Acres. The object had been to give the seniors something to look forward to beyond Sunday visits from their children. Especially since most of them spent Sunday waiting for children who often got too busy with their own lives to show up.

She knew the feeling.

She'd spent many nights waiting for her mother to come home. Half the time she hadn't shown up at all and the other half, she'd stumbled in with a cowboy on her arm. Either way, she'd been too busy for Miranda.

Too busy falling into lust.

Cody's image pushed into her head, his eyes a brilliant, sparkling purple, his fangs glittering in the moonlight. He'd wanted so much to bite her, yet he'd held back. She'd felt it in the tension of his muscles and the fierceness of his touch.

So? That's a good thing.

She knew that. At the same time, she couldn't help but wonder why. Because she wasn't attractive enough? Sexy enough?

Bingo.

It only made sense. She'd spent a lifetime suppressing her sexy side. Maybe she'd finally buried it so deep that there was no unearthing it now. Maybe she'd been so determined to turn out different from her mother and sisters that she'd gone too far in the other direction.

If only that thought didn't bother her almost as much as the notion of following in her mother's footsteps.

She ignored the strange push-pull inside of her and turned her attention back to the table full of seniors to her left. The Rolling Romeos—a duo of old men who prided themselves on dancing with every female whenever the center held a big "shindig"—were about to take their turn. One clutched the dice fiercely while the other chanted, "Come on, Earl. You can do it. Just shake off the arthritis and let 'er rip."

"Hey, there, Mr. Hartford," Miranda said as she came up to them carrying the platter of cinnamon rolls.

The old man paused to give Miranda a wink. "Howdy, little lady." He blew on his closed fist and threw his hands forward. The dice hit and rolled. He high-fived his

partner while the other two men at the table—the Geri-
atric Gringos—booed and clacked their dentures.

"You old cheat, Earl," one of them cackled.

"Ain't no cheating involved. That there's skill."

"Says you."

"We're just better than you, George," Earl's partner
said as he reached for the dice. "You might as well
climb down off your high horse and admit it…"

Bickering. One-upmanship. All was right at Golden
Acres.

Miranda finished replenishing the cinnamon rolls
and set the remaining platter on a nearby refreshment
table. "Orange juice?" she asked a white-haired lady
humming past her in a motorized wheelchair.

"Only if it's got a little extra kick." Martha Louise
McCall swerved to a stop and smiled, revealing a row
of bright white dentures.

"What did I tell you about drinking and driving,
Martha? Last time you drank mimosas for Harriet
Sandford's birthday party, you took out the bird bath in
the courtyard."

"And it was the most excitement we've had around
here since Dora Lee Strunk got arrested for indecent
exposure when the elastic on her Depends broke and she
mooned the men's choir during the Christmas pageant."

Miranda barely resisted the grin that tugged at her
lips. "Dora Lee didn't think it was funny."

"Yeah, well she's got a stick up her keister. Speaking
of which," Martha motioned to the woman pushing a
metallic blue walker. "Hey, there, Dora Lee. You
playing this morning?"

"And send my sugar sky high?" The old woman gave a loud *harrumph*. "Those cinnamon rolls are poison, I tell you. We ought to be playing for something useful. Like some Dr. Scholl footpads or a bottle of Mylanta."

"The membership voted for cinnamon rolls," Miranda reminded the woman. "It won almost unanimously. We only had two write-ins. One for Mylanta and one for Cosmopolitans."

The old woman snorted and gave Miranda the evil eye. "I knew the moment they hired a Rivers to run things around here that we'd all be going to hell in a handbasket."

The words grazed old wounds and reminded Miranda of the time she'd been on the playground and one of the girls had thrown a volleyball at her. *"Rivers, Rivers. You're a no good Rivers."*

"It doesn't matter what everyone else thinks." Cody's words echoed in Miranda's head and oddly enough, Dora Lee's remarks didn't sting the way they usually did.

"You ought to take up motivational speaking, Dora Lee." Martha smiled. "Spread the joy with that stellar personality of yours."

Dora Lee wagged a finger. "You're every bit the heathen she is."

"A Cosmopolitan-drinking heathen and damned proud of it."

"You're both going to hell," Dora Lee muttered. "Straight down, no detours."

"Just so long as they have in-flight cocktails," Martha called out as the woman waddled away. "Don't let her bother you," she told Miranda. "She's just mad because she wasn't the one who got lucky last night."

Miranda became instantly aware of the tingling on her face courtesy of Cody's stubble-roughed face. "I, um, used this new face cream and it must have irritated my skin."

"I'm not talking about you, sweetie, though the good Lord knows you could use a little cayenne pepper in your life. I'm talking about me." She beamed. "I beat the pants off Nicki and Jake at last night's poker game."

Sunday was poker night at the center. Another brainstorm Miranda had come up with to divert attention from the fact that Sunday was visiting day. Miranda attended every once in a while, but since she spent five days a week plus every other Saturday at Golden Acres, she usually opted out of poker night to plan her weekly schedule. That, and she'd all but lost her shirt the last time she'd gone up against Jeanine Picklebaker, a ninety-three-year-old once-upon-a-time blackjack dealer from Vegas. The woman gave new meaning to the word "card shark."

"Not literally, mind you," Martha went on. "Otherwise I would have had another heart attack for sure. My old ticker ain't what it used to be. 'Specially if there's a naked man involved. Anyhow, I got big time lucky at poker last night and I've got a whole jar full of lemon drops to prove it. Plus a lifetime supply of motor oil for my wheelchair. Jake promised to do the change himself, and throw in new spark plugs."

Miranda eyed the motorized chair. "You have spark plugs on that thing?"

"I haven't got a clue, but it gives me the opportunity to pay a visit to Skull Creek Choppers and indulge in some serious eye candy. Why, if that man weren't already taken, I'd introduce him to my granddaughter Jenny."

"The accountant?"

"Unfortunately. I swear, that girl wouldn't know exciting if it jumped up and bit her in the backside. Do you know what she got me for grandparents day last year? A coupon to get my taxes done for free."

"It sounds practical."

"That's the problem. She needs some serious eye candy to sweeten up things." She wagged a bony finger at Miranda. "That goes for you, too."

"Greg is eye candy."

"Greg is a Tic Tac. I'm talking a Goo Goo Cluster. Sweet, yummy and dee-licious."

Miranda's lips tingled and she remembered the taste of Cody's mouth on hers. Sweet. Forbidden. *Dee-licious*.

She cleared her suddenly dry throat. "I really should get more orange juice," she blurted, desperate to change the subject and push Cody out of her head.

It was just sex, she reminded herself. No letting him get under her skin and into her head. Her heart. *No*.

Holding tight to the thought, she refilled the orange juice container and checked to make sure that the kitchen still had enough cinnamon rolls for the play-off round. After that, she headed for her office and the pile of work that waited for her.

Work was good.

Distracting.

She powered up her computer and spent the next half

hour finalizing the details for Friday night's sock hop. She finished the menu, ordered the food and sent an e-mail confirmation to Bob Waller, one of Skull Creek's finest who moonlighted his security services at various functions around town—the VFW spaghetti night, the town fair, the Ladies Who Pray annual clothing swap. She was just sending a reminder to the disc jockey—complete with a request for Fats Domino's "Blueberry Hill"—when her inbox gave a loud *bleep*. The username *cleanfreak223* blazed back at her and she debated whether or not to click on the message. It was Greg.

What if he wanted an answer now?

She wasn't sure why the notion suddenly bothered her. It wasn't as if Cody was going to stick around. He was a vampire, for heaven's sake. He didn't have relationships with women. He had sex and sucked their blood. End of story.

Other women, that is, except for her.

He only had sex with her. No blood-sucking involved.

She ignored the spiral of jealousy that went through her and opened Greg's e-mail.

The conference is going good. I've got a whole suitcase full of spot remover samples. I even won the nightly drawing for five hundred free hangers. Can't wait to get back and start using some of this stuff. Speaking of getting back, I was thinking we could forget a long engagement and go ahead and tie the knot at city park. That way we won't have to waste a ton of money on flowers. We can have the reception at The Hungry Pig barbecue. They've got a buffet special that includes ribs, fried alligator and macaroni salad. The pecan pie will save us from having to buy a wedding cake. We're going to keep it simple.

And cheap.

The thought struck, followed by a wave of guilt. Greg wasn't cheap. He was practical. Safe. Perfect.

Even if he didn't want a wedding cake.

Not that she was one of those women who spent countless hours envisioning her own wedding. She didn't. But she'd sort of counted on at least a wedding cake. Something small and tasteful. Maybe with a few sugar roses. Roses were her favorite, after all, and Greg knew that.

But they weren't *his* favorite.

He liked daisies and so he always brought daisies for special occasions. He liked to garden and so they spent every Sunday gardening. He liked to have meatloaf at the diner every Friday and so they had a standing reservation even though Miranda didn't really like meatloaf.

"It's the best meatloaf in the county," he'd told her too many times to count. *"You have to eat it."*

And so she had.

The way she'd done everything else he'd said—from gardening to listening to jazz to giving up linen because it was a bitch to clean and polyester blends were so much easier. She'd wanted to please him. To be good enough for him.

Because she hadn't been good enough for her mother.

The thought pushed its way in and she pushed it right back out.

This wasn't about her past. It was about her future. A different future. She wanted to change things. She already had. She'd earned the love of a good man.

She eyeballed the e-mail. There were no terms of endearments. No *I miss you so much* or *I can't wait to see you again.* Not even a simple *Love, Greg.*

Because he didn't love her.

A spiral of relief shot through her. A crazy reaction considering this wasn't about love. They were a good match. She wanted reliable and practical and safe, and Greg was all three. He was perfect and she *was* marrying him.

Then do it. Say yes.

She clicked on Reply. Her fingers touched the keyboard and Cody's image pushed into her head.

Not the sexy picture he'd made last night sitting bucknaked in the seat of the John Deere. No, she saw him standing in front of her, fully clothed, his eyes a deep, mesmerizing blue. His voice filled with conviction as he murmured, *"It doesn't matter what other people think."*

Her heart skipped its next beat and a strange warmth spread through her. It was a feeling that had nothing to do with lust and everything to do with the sense of camaraderie she'd felt with him during those last few moments at the feed store.

She typed in a quick *Great!* and hit Send.

What? It was a marriage proposal, for Pete's sake. She wasn't going to say yes via e-mail.

That's what she told herself as she turned back to work on the schedule for tomorrow's activities.

She just wasn't one hundred percent sure she still believed it.

18

THE SOUND OF KNOCKING POUNDED through the blackness that engulfed Cody. He pushed his eyes open and forced himself to his feet. His muscles felt heavy, tired. He knew it wasn't even noon before he glanced at the clock. Sun peeked around the edges of the blinds and sucked at his strength, but he made it to the door anyway.

"Yeah?"

"It's Eldin, Mr. Boyd. Eldin Atkins. Remember me from check-in? Can I talk to you for a second?"

Cody threw the lock on the door and pulled it open a half-inch. Light spilled through the opening and he shrank back into the safety of the shadows. A split second later, Eldin leaned closer and peered into the inch-wide space, effectively blocking the rays.

"Just thought I'd let you know that there was someone here looking for you last night. Tall. Dark hair. Smart mouth. Said he was a reporter for some rodeo magazine. I think his name was Lenny—"

"Benny?" Cody stiffened. "Benny James?"

"That's it."

Shit.

Obviously James hadn't bought the story Cody had fed him about passing through town. He'd followed him here.

Shit. Shit. *Shit.*

"Anyhow, I just wanted to let you know that I took care of everything for you. I told him if he was looking for the infamous Cody Boyd, he was looking in the wrong place 'cause we don't got no famous rodeo cowboys staying here in the VIP suite. And we sure as hell don't have any famous rodeo cowboys here that don't want to be disturbed."

"I appreciate that."

"My pleasure. Just so's you know, I've got my lawn chair right here just to make sure he don't pull no funny business and try to get past me."

"I really appreciate that, Eldin, but don't you think it might look a little bit suspicious? You sitting in front of the VIP door with a shotgun?"

"I didn't really think about that. Maybe I'll skedaddle down a few doors and throw him off the track."

"Or you could head back to the lobby and play it cool like nothing is going on. Then he might be inclined to think I'm staying at one of the motels out on the interstate."

"I *could* monitor things from inside with my binoculars."

"Sounds like a plan."

"If I see any funny business, I can get on the horn. I've got Sheriff Keller's number pre-programmed in my cell. One touch and this place'll be crawling with cops."

Cody seriously doubted a town the size of Skull Creek had more than two or three full-time officers, so *crawling* was definite overkill. But he wasn't going to rain on Eldin's parade. The man was on a roll.

"'Cause no guest of mine is gonna be bothered by no annoying reporters. You came here 'cause you need your peace and quiet. The least I can do is guaran-damn-tee that ain't nobody gonna bother you. 'Sides, I told you that I'm used to famous celebrities here. We get 'em all the time here. Speaking of famous celebrities, you okay on clean towels? 'Cause I'd be happy to bring you extra—"

"Fine," Cody cut in. "I'm doing just fine."

"How about ice? I'd be happy to head over to the ice machine and—"

"I'm good on ice, too, buddy."

"Clean sheets?"

"Winona changed them yesterday."

"A new Bible?"

"Still got one right here in the top drawer. Listen, thanks a lot for all you're doing. I really appreciate it."

"Anytime." Eldin smiled and turned to fold up his lawn chair.

Cody shut and locked the door and stumbled back to the bed. Collapsing on the mattress, he let his eyes close and did his damnedest not to think about Benny James.

So what if the man had followed him here? He'd been following him forever and Cody had managed to stay one step ahead. He would do the same now. He simply had to watch his back and keep a low profile for the next four days until Sawyer returned.

And bumping and grinding on the fifty-yard line of the local stadium was obviously the way to do it.

His thoughts shifted to Miranda and his nostrils flared. The sticky sweet smell of cinnamon teased his senses and the clatter of dice echoed in his ears. She was supervising the morning activities at the senior center, going about her normal routine, determined to distract herself and pretend like this was any other Monday.

It wasn't.

Anticipation rippled through her, making her hands tremble and her knees weak. The memories from the previous night followed her, sneaking into her conscious thoughts whenever she wasn't looking and stirring her lust.

He glanced down at the erection tenting the sheets. He knew the feeling.

He rolled onto his side and tried to think about something else. About Benny James and the danger he posed should he get even a glimpse of the truth. About the coming confrontation with Garret Sawyer and the need for revenge that ate away inside of him. About the bull he'd pulled for the first round of the season. An ornery bitch named Jolene that would surely give him the ride of his afterlife.

Then again, he'd already had that last night.

The thought struck, teasing his senses and turning his attention to the sounds and smells and feelings that surrounded him.

The sensations intensified as the hours wore on. An unbelievable fact because daylight never failed to zap his strength and dull his senses.

But while his muscles lay heavy and catatonic, his brain was fully tuned.

He'd felt her since that morning. Her excitement at arriving at the senior center to find a cup of hot coffee waiting for her courtesy of one of the residents. Her disappointment when some little old lady had bad-mouthed her. Her angst over whether or not to serve mini pizzas or the ever-popular pigs-in-a-blanket. Her displeasure when she'd opened her e-mail.

He stiffened and jealousy bolted through him, as strong and resilient as when he'd first felt it that morning. Friggin' crazy, he knew. But it was there.

As if he cared that she was so determined to ruin the rest of her life and marry someone else. She wouldn't be happy. A truth that didn't matter one way or another to him.

Yeah, right. And all you need is a little SPF and you'll be fine outdoors.

All right, so he did care. He finally admitted that to himself as the day wore on and the feelings intensified.

Not that he was going to do anything about it. He was in Skull Creek for one reason only—to kill Garret Sawyer the way he should have done that tragic night, rid himself of the damned what-ifs and find a little peace of mind.

He damned sure wasn't here because of a woman. And he double damned sure wasn't staying because of one. Sure, it might sound good just thinking about it. Maybe buying a few acres and building a house and planting some roots. But he knew from personal experience that it would lose its appeal like everything else. That's why he kept moving.

That's where he and his dad had been different.

His father had slowed down and let a woman fall in love with him, and then he'd broken her heart and abandoned his boys.

Cody wasn't making that mistake. He might not be able to help the restlessness, but he could sure as hell keep from hurting someone else.

He could walk away.

He would.

But until then he had a touchdown to score.

MIRANDA SAT IN THE FRONT ROW of the bleachers at Skull Creek High football stadium and tried to calm the frantic beat of her heart. At the rate she was going, she'd die of a heart attack before he even arrived.

She drew a steady breath, willed her nerves to chill and concentrated on her surroundings. The only light came from the full moon that hung in an otherwise pitch black sky. The white field paint gleamed in the celestial light, marking the various yard lines. Her gaze riveted on the fifty and she remembered the first time she'd seen it written on the boy's bathroom wall.

Before the embarrassment and mortification, she'd felt the tiniest, most illicit thrill. A reaction she'd buried and forgotten until now.

Now, the sensation spiraled through her, prickling her skin and pebbling her nipples and—

"Penny for your thoughts." His deep voice drew her attention. Her head snapped to the left and she found him sitting beside her just a few inches away.

He wore a black Stetson tipped low over his forehead so that it shrouded the upper half of his face and made him seem even more dark and dangerous and sexy. A black Ride 'Em Cowboy T-shirt clung to his broad chest and accented his heavily muscled biceps. Faded jeans hugged his muscular thighs, the frayed ends bunched just above a pair of worn black boots.

He grinned, the expression a slash of white in the darkness. "Thinking about old times?"

"Hardly." She swallowed against her suddenly dry throat. "I was more the geeky math club type." She grinned as she remembered the small group of friends she'd made back then. They'd been the only people who hadn't judged her. But then she'd had every algebraic equation memorized and so they'd needed her for the academic decathlon. "I went to exactly one football game my entire life and I left at half time."

He slid closer until barely an inch separated them. "Not much of a football fan?"

"I'm actually a huge Cowboys fan. I coordinate a game trip to Dallas every year. The residents love it." She shook her head. "My lack of team spirit back in high school had nothing to do with the game." She wasn't sure why she told him. With his vampire senses, he undoubtedly knew. At the same time, he looked so interested, that she couldn't help herself. "It was freshman year. First scrimmage. Trisha Rhinehart accused me of flirting with her boyfriend. He dropped his wallet after paying for popcorn at the concession stand. I was standing behind him in line, so I picked it up and handed it back to him. Big mistake. When Trisha came out of the restroom and saw us talking, she flipped. She said I was no better than my white trash mother and sisters. I left. That was my first and last time here."

"She sounds really insecure."

"I don't blame her." She shrugged. "Matt was always cheating on her."

"But not with you."

She shook her head. "No, but there was no way for Trisha to know that. I don't blame her for jumping to conclusions. My mother was the town whore before she died, and my sisters are still following in her footsteps."

"You're not your sisters."

Yeah, right.

His thigh brushed hers and heat swept from her toes to the top of her head. She was just as lusty. Just as wanton. She just controlled it and they didn't.

"What about you?" she heard herself blurt despite her vow not to ask him any questions. She needed something—anything—to fill the tense silence and distract herself from the erotic urges pushing and pulling inside of her, threatening her sanity and her precious control.

Forget waiting until the fifty-yard line. She saw herself peeling off her clothes and straddling his lap and—

"Any sisters?" she rushed on. Her hands trembled and her lips quivered. "Brothers?"

He stiffened and she knew she'd hit on a subject he'd rather not talk about. "No sisters," he finally said after a long moment, "but I do have three older brothers. Brent, Travis and Colton."

"Do they live in Texas?"

He shrugged. "I can't say as I know. We see each other once a year, but we don't talk much."

"Bad blood?"

"Something like that."

"Must be some family reunion."

He grinned and the tension in his body eased just a fraction. "It's not that kind of reunion. Every year on the anniversary of his turning, a vampire must return to the actual spot where he took his last breath as a man. We were all turned at our family's ranch, so we go home every year." He stared off into the distance. "But it isn't much of a home anymore. The entire place fell into ruin after my family was killed. All of the buildings were destroyed by fire. Nothing was ever rebuilt. It's just a grassy stretch of pasture now." He stared out at the football field. "When I see it, it's hard to believe that it was once one of the biggest spreads in West Texas."

Don't do it. Don't ask. "What happened?" The words tumbled past her lips anyway. There was just something about the frown pinching his brow that made her want to ask. To listen.

A welcome urge compared to the lustful ones warring with her sanity, threatening her precious control.

"My brothers and I were on our way back after the war. We arrived to find the ranch blazing and everyone dead or nearly so. I found my mother a few seconds before she took her last breath." Pain drew his mouth tight.

A feeling she was all too familiar with.

"It's terrible to see anyone die."

He nodded. "The rest of the family—my sister-in-law, my ten-year-old nephew—they were both killed. The ranch hands. Our foreman. Most of our horses were caught in the fire, too. There wasn't a thing left standing."

"What about your father?"

He stiffened. "He was never in the picture. He left us a long time ago. The wanderlust, my ma used to call it, but she was just making excuses for him. He wasn't very dependable."

"My father wasn't in the picture either. My sisters and I all have different dads. I've never even met mine."

"I don't waste much time wishing he'd been around, but I do wish he'd been there that night. Maybe things would have been different."

"I'm really sorry for your loss. It must have been terrible for you."

"You can't imagine."

But she could. She could see the horrific images that haunted his thoughts and she could feel his pain.

And her own.

"I found my mother after she'd taken a handful of pills," she heard herself say. "I called 911, but it was too late. By the time they got there, she was dead." She could still hear the clatter of the empty pill bottle as it hit the linoleum, the shrill whine of the sirens, then the silence once the police had cleared out and she'd sat there with a social worker waiting for her older sisters.

"Why she'd do it?"

"She fell for this guy, but he didn't fall for her. He was a truck driver. Turns out he had a wife in Houston and four kids. My mother couldn't take the rejection and so she gave up. She was always giving up. When she couldn't make ends meet, she'd head for the nearest bar and drink away her troubles. Then she'd head home with some man for a few more hours of distraction. But the problems were always waiting for her the next day."

We were waiting.

"I'm sorry."

She'd heard the sentiment so many times over the years. Sometimes sincere. Sometimes not. But never had it soothed the hurt deep inside her.

It didn't now, she told herself. But she felt the slightest bit of relief anyway. Her chest didn't feel as tight, her heart as pinched. Understanding gleamed in his eyes and for the first time since her mother had died, she didn't feel quite so alone.

"So what about you?" he asked suddenly as if he'd sensed the camaraderie and he wasn't all that happy about it. "Why are you here?"

"I was born here."

"I mean *here*." He glanced around. "Tell me about Mr. Perfect."

"Well." She licked her lips and searched for the right words when all she wanted to do was to turn and kiss him. "We're both Lean and Mean Buckee Breakfast eaters."

A grin tugged at his mouth. "I'll probably hate myself for asking this, but what the hell is a Buckee Breakfast eater?"

"The diner serves five different sized breakfast entrees. There's the Buckee Grande, the Buckee not-so-grande, the Buckee lean-and-mean and the Buckee is-this-all-the-hell-there-is?" When he arched an eyebrow, she added, "No, really. That's exactly what it says on the menu. Anyhow, the most popular is the Buckee Grande, and it's all downhill from there. I usually order the last one which consists of wheat toast because I'm dieting." Because everything—repeat *everything*—went straight to her hips.

"I think your hips are perfect."

"So sayeth the sex-crazed vampire," she told him, despite the sliver of warmth that stole through her. A feeling that had nothing to do with the lust and everything to do with the conviction in his voice. "Anyhow, I stopped off at the diner on my way to work about six months ago and ordered my usual. They got my order mixed up with someone else who'd ordered the same thing. I wouldn't have known, but I always get the orange marmalade and they gave me apple butter. Anyhow, that's how Greg and I met. He came back in for his apple butter and I went back for my marmalade. We recognized each other from high school and started talking."

"So you were friends way back when?"

"I knew who he was and he knew who I was, but I was Restroom Randy and his daddy was the newly elected mayor. Friendship was out of the question. After graduation, he headed for Houston to make his way in the world while I stayed here and worked my way through junior college. When our orders got mixed up at the diner he'd just moved back here. His dad was sick and so he came home to take over the family's dry cleaning business. His dad passed away and so now he runs things permanently. I get free steam cleaning."

"Lucky you."

"I know it's not the most exciting job, but it's a nice, respectable way to make a living. Greg's a great guy."

"If he was all that, then you wouldn't be here."

Amen.

She ignored the traitorous thought and tightened her defenses. "There are more important things than sex. We have a lot in common. We both volunteer at the local library. We love old Westerns and chai tea and gardening. He raises prizewinning Gerber daisies and—"

"Let me guess—daisies are your favorite flower."

"Not exactly. I'm partial to roses, but you're missing the point. I like flowers and so does he. And we both like shrimp cocktail and bingo and eighties music."

"Sounds like a love match, all right."

"Actually, it has nothing to do with love. I can count on Greg. He isn't like all the other jerks out there." He wasn't the kind of guy who walked away as soon as the deed was done.

He wasn't Cody Braddock.

That thought should have made her feel relieved. Instead, she felt a moment of regret so profound that it tightened her chest and made her swallow.

But then Cody's thigh brushed hers again and the feeling faded in a wave of heat so intense it robbed the air from her lungs.

As undependable as Cody was, there was one thing she could rely on him for—the one thing she wanted right now.

Another delicious orgasm.

"We should really get started." She pushed to her feet and started across the row of bleachers toward the staircase that led down onto the field. "We've only got a few days and six more locations after tonight. I was thinking we could get started a little earlier tomorrow night, maybe eight, and do a double feature. The gazebo first and then the library—"

"Sounds like a plan," Cody's voice cut in and drew her attention just as she was descending the steps.

Her head snapped up and she found him standing smack dab in the middle of the fifty-yard line, his brilliant purple eyes blazing like neon lights in the darkness.

"Take off your clothes." His voice was gruff, sexy, mesmerizing.

Her fingers itched and she came so close to reaching for the hem of her shirt. She balled her hands and concentrated on breathing as she cleared the steps and crossed the distance to him. "You first," she managed as she stopped just a few feet away.

He looked oddly disappointed that she didn't obey, but then the expression faded into pure, seductive intent and Miranda couldn't escape the feeling that she'd somehow made a huge mistake.

She'd drawn a line in the sand and she had the sudden feeling that Cody Braddock was about to do everything in his power to make her cross it.

Starting right now.

19

HE WASN'T GOING TO TOUCH her first.

Cody made that promise to himself as he faced off with Miranda on the football field. Moonlight bathed her features, accenting the dips and curves of her luscious body clothed in the simple white button-up blouse and black skirt she'd worn to work that day. She looked anything but wild and wicked at that moment, but he knew better.

He could feel the lust that ebbed and flowed through her. Even more, he could see it in the brightness of her eyes and the trembling of her full lips and the clenching of her hands. She was struggling, fighting to ignore what lived and breathed inside of her.

A losing battle.

She was too sexy a woman to live her entire life bottling it all up. She needed to let it out. To let go. To give up her precious control and embrace her wild side, at least once. That's why he wasn't going to touch her first. At least not with his hands.

His mind, however, was a different story altogether.

He focused his gaze on the smooth column of her throat and reached out.

She felt the purposeful caress and shock jolted

through her for a split second. It was a reaction that had nothing to do with the fact that he was standing yards away, touching her in ways no man ever could, and everything to do with the fact that she liked it. Too much.

He watched the war of emotions on her face—pleasure going head-to-head with fear, desperation versus desire—and his determination fired hotter, brighter.

Goosebumps chased the lengths of her arms. Her nipples ripened, pushing tight against the material of her blouse. He shifted his attention lower, to the modest skirt that hit her well below the knee.

He moved his hand and the button at her waist slid free. The zipper slithered down and the skirt worked its way down her hips and legs, to her feet. Her white cotton panties quickly followed.

His attention focused on the vee between her legs. The hair had been trimmed and waxed into a neat little strip that stirred his lust and made him forget his objective for one tense, teeth-gripping moment. The urge to shove her down to the ground and plunge fast and deep into her hot body nearly overwhelmed him.

But then, that's what she wanted. She wanted him to take the lead, the responsibility. Then she wouldn't have to face the fact that she wanted him of her own accord.

He stood his ground and forced himself to get a grip on the hunger raging inside of him. He took a deep breath into his lungs and then let it out slowly. The rush of air carried to her, whispering over her bare flesh and teasing the tender folds between her legs.

He smelled the rush of wetness and felt the sharp tightening of her clitoris.

A nod of his head and the buttons on her blouse started to pop free one by one until the edges parted, revealing a white lace bra.

The blouse slithered down her arms and fell on top of the panties. Her nipples grew tight and hard, eager to be stroked and nibbled. Anticipation coiled inside her.

He reached out and his thumb grazed the very tip of her breast through the lace of her bra. "You're so beautiful." The moment he said the words, she felt the clasp give. The straps sagged on her shoulders. The cups fell away and just like that, he was actually touching her, the rough pad of his thumb rasping the sensitive nub. The pressure, sharp and sweet, tightened between her legs and she stiffened.

"You don't have to fight so hard." His deep voice slid into Miranda's ears, skimmed her senses and stirred her body that much more. His gaze collided with hers. *"Stop running and let go."*

She wanted to, she realized in a rush of heat so intense that it sucked the air from her lungs and stalled her heart for a long, endless moment. She wanted to give herself up to the need gripping her body. Lose herself in the sensation swamping her senses. Fully. Completely.

She'd never done that. Sex had always come with angst. With the worry that if she gave too much or went too far, she wouldn't be able to pull herself back. She'd fall head over heels into the lust and it would suck her under the way it had her mother.

But greater than that worry was the thought that she might never feel this way again. Cody was the first man to ever make her feel so alive and she knew deep down that he would be the last. Vampire or not, he was one of a kind.

And temporary.

He would walk away soon and she would be left with only her memories of him. Of this moment.

He lifted his own arms then and his T-shirt slithered up and over his head, as if invisible hands pushed it from his hard, muscular body. The button on his jeans popped and the zipper worked its way down. The jeans sagged on his hips and his erection sprang hot and greedy toward her.

"Touch me."

The command, so desperate and gruff, called to something deep inside her and suddenly she could no more hold back than she could stop breathing.

She touched the tip before sliding her hand down his length, stroking, exploring. His dark flesh throbbed against her palm and her own body shuddered. Forget the actual sex. She wanted to drop to her knees and take him into her mouth, suck him, taste him.

The urge hit her hard and fast and for the first time, Miranda didn't fight it. She dropped to her knees and reached for him.

She flicked her tongue and caught the drop of pearly liquid that beaded on the ripe purple head. His essence exploded on her tongue, so sweet and salty. Her own hunger stirred and she drew him into her mouth, stroking and laving and relishing the feel of him throbbing against her tongue.

She loved him with her mouth as he splayed his

fingers through her hair and cradled her head. She pleasured him until his fingers clenched and his gruff voice echoed in her ears.

"Don't."

Because women didn't pleasure Cody Braddock. He pleasured women.

That's the way it had always been for him with every woman and he wasn't the least bit anxious for a change.

Regret welled inside of Miranda and her throat tightened. While she'd recognized that he was different from all the other men in her past, to him she was just one of the crowd. A quick lay. A fast meal—

"No." His deep voice cut into her mental tirade as he drew her to her feet. "You're more than that, Miranda. I've never wanted a woman as much as I want you."

Desire blazed in his eyes, along with a gleam of conviction that melted her insecurities. Just like that, she stopped thinking and worrying and being afraid.

Rather, she stepped forward. And this time, *she* kissed *him.*

Her tongue tangled with his and she gave herself up to the feel of his mouth on hers. Sliding her arms around his neck, she held him close. She pressed her body against his, feeling the hard length of his frame.

It was the hottest kiss of her life, and it got even hotter when he turned the tables on her and took the lead.

He licked his way down her neck, her collarbone, and pleasure rushed to her brain. Her balance seemed to give way and she became lightheaded.

He arched her back and his lips caught her nipple.

She buried her hands in his hair, holding him close, arching her breast into the moist heat of his mouth as he suckled her.

"Open your eyes," he murmured after a long, delicious moment.

Miranda did as he commanded and suddenly the dizzy, weightless feeling made sense. She glanced down to see ground far below. They hovered in midair high above the fifty yard line.

Panic swamped her, followed by a wave of desire as he caught her bottom and lifted her. In one swift thrust, he plunged deep. Her thoughts shattered and suddenly falling to her death was the furthest thing from her mind. The only thing she could think of in that next moment was feeling him closer. Deeper.

She clung to him, wrapping her legs around him and moving just enough until he was buried even more fully inside of her. The delicious fullness sent jolts of electricity chasing up and down the length of her spine. Grasping at his shoulders, she held on tight as he cupped her buttocks and urged her to move. He slid her up and down, working her, over and over. Harder and faster.

When she felt the first wave of pleasure, she dug her nails into his flesh and held on as sensation rocked her body. It was the sweetest, most wonderful orgasm to date and she caught her lip against the exquisite sensation. Her head fell back and she clamped her eyes shut. Heat drenched her and stole the breath from her lungs.

His groan, so pained and desperate, slid past the thunder of her own heart and she forced her eyes open.

His eyes fired a wild, vibrant purple. The tendons in

his neck tightened. His jaw clenched. His mouth fell open and his fangs gleamed in the dim light.

Regret hit her as she wondered if he would follow through this time, along with a niggle of fear that he wouldn't. But then his mouth closed over the side of her neck where her pulse beat a frantic rhythm and he sank his fangs deliciously deep.

There was no pain, just a smart prickle followed by a flood of *wow* that drenched her senses and consumed her. A gasp trembled up her throat.

And then he added fuel to the fire by thrusting into her, pushing deep with his body while he drew on her with his mouth. The double dose of sensation was unlike anything she'd ever experienced before. She grasped at his shoulders, holding on and riding the flood of pleasure. He drove her mindless, working her up all over again as if she hadn't just had the most incredible orgasm of her life. She had, but it didn't matter because this was better.

Sharper.

Sweeter.

She cried out, splintering into a thousand pieces. Her body tightened around him and he stiffened. He came then in a rush of bubbling warmth. His arms tightened. His body bucked. His teeth sank deeper, coaxing a few more sweet drops of blood as he spilled himself inside of her.

His mouth eased and he buried his head against her neck as she clung to him, savoring the tremors that rocked them both.

Slowly, her heartbeat calmed and the dizzy feeling subsided. She opened her eyes just as they reached the ground. He loosened his hold and eased her down the length of his hard body.

The reality of what had just happened settled in as she stared up at him and saw the surprise and disbelief warring in his gaze. He stared at the prick points on her neck as if he couldn't believe what he'd done.

As if he couldn't forgive himself.

"Shit," he finally murmured. "Holy *shit*." And then he did the one thing Miranda had feared her entire life.

He left her staring after him and walked away.

HE BIT HER.

The truth followed Cody to his pick-up truck and dogged him as he gunned the engine and peeled out of the parking lot, racing hell for leather back to the motel that sat a few blocks away.

He had to get away.

From her.

From the damnable knowledge that he'd just made a huge mistake.

Of all the stupid, crazy, irresponsible, *predictable* things.

He hadn't been able to help himself.

She'd surrendered to him, unleashing her wild side, and it had just been too much.

He'd been so wrapped up in his own feelings, so hot and turned on and hungry, that he'd forgotten the reasons why biting her was such a bad idea. He'd said to hell with the repercussions and drank from her anyway.

And now the damage was done. The connection forged. The bond unbreakable.

The sticky sweetness of her blood lingered on his tongue and his gut clenched. His pulse raced. He could still feel the delicious heat gliding down his throat, fire-bombing his stomach. More potent than anything he'd ever tasted. More addictive.

Even now, miles away, he wanted more.

But not just her blood. He wanted her uninhibited and uncontrollable in his arms every night. He wanted her sleeping beside him every day. He wanted to talk to her and spend time with her and see her smile the way she had tonight when she'd mentioned the math club. He wanted forever.

He slammed on his brakes, swerved into the parking lot of the motel and sat there. Engine idling. Thoughts racing. His knuckles white on the steering wheel as the truth hit him like a two-by-four upside the head.

He loved her.

He felt it pushing and pulling inside of him, waging a battle far more violent than the hunger. He wanted to shove the truck into Reverse, pull out onto Main Street, haul ass back to her, sweep her up into his arms and never let go.

He wanted *her,* from this day forward, forever and ever.

But she wanted something far different.

He could feel the tears slipping down her cheeks, the anguish as she sat on the bleachers, listening for the sound of his truck. She sat there and waited for him to turn around, to come back, hoping against hope that he wasn't like every other man.

He wasn't.

He was worse because he wasn't a man.

He couldn't piddle around the garden with her or take her to the weekly church picnic or cuddle up next to her on her front porch swing and watch the sun set. He couldn't be the stability she so desperately needed, and he sure as hell couldn't promise her a future.

He was facing off with Garret Sawyer in less than three days. A fight to the death. And while Cody had every intention of winning, he couldn't guarantee it.

He might not make it.

Christ, he couldn't guarantee he'd be around next week, much less forever, and he knew she wouldn't settle for anything less.

Because she wasn't her mother.

She might be as lustful, but that's where the similarity ended. She was stronger. More compassionate. She cared about other people. The people at the senior center. Her sisters. While they didn't have the most ideal relationship, she was still there for them, helping them out when they needed her.

She made it her business to be there for everyone else, and so she deserved the same. Someone she could count on. Someone who wasn't limited by the darkness.

Someone other than Cody.

He killed the engine and climbed out of the truck. He made it two steps before the prickling awareness hit him.

All thought faded as his body tensed and his muscles tightened and his survival instincts kicked in. His fangs sharpened and a growl vibrated his vocal chords.

And then Cody turned to face the vampire that stood directly behind him.

20

"CHILL, BRO."

The deep, familiar voice slithered into Cody's ears a split second before he found himself staring at his past.

Brent Braddock held up his hands. "Easy." He crossed the few feet that separated them. "I'm not going to hurt you."

"As if you could."

A grin tugged at the older vampire's lips. "You have a short memory, otherwise you'd distinctly remember the time I hog-tied you and hung you from that magnolia tree."

Before they'd been turned.

The mention of the past tugged at something soft inside Cody and for a split second, the wall that had erected between him and his brothers that fateful night seemed to crumble just a little.

Staring at Brent Braddock was like staring at a slightly older version of himself. His brother had the same dark hair, the same angular jaw, the same broad shoulders and muscular body. The only thing different was his eyes. They were a pale, translucent green.

He dressed different, too. He wore black leather pants, a fitted black button-down shirt—the ends untucked—

and gleaming black Roper boots. He looked every bit one of those big city types playing at being a real cowboy. But Cody knew better.

Brent was hard-core. He could ride. Rope. Shoot. The Braddock boys had been the fastest guns in the Confederacy, but Brent had always been a little bit faster. A little more dangerous. A lot more reckless.

While Cody had a wild streak, Brent had an I-don't-give-a-shit attitude that made him much more lethal. To others and himself. A trait that had wiped out the loyalty he'd once felt to his brothers and taken over completely once he'd been turned.

Cody flashed back to one of the many times he and his brothers had sat by the campfire, plotting their next raid, sharing their thoughts, sharing themselves.

They'd had each other's backs. A band of brothers. *Once.*

Bitterness welled inside of him and his chest tightened. He turned, walked the few feet toward his motel door and shoved the keycard into the slot.

"What are you doing here?" he asked when Brent came up behind him.

"I'm here to kill Sawyer."

Cody pushed open the door and walked inside. "I didn't realize he had a bounty on his head."

"He doesn't." Brent followed him in and kicked the door shut. "I'm doing this for free."

Flipping on a light, Cody turned on his brother. "You don't do anything for free."

Brent shrugged and sprawled in a nearby chair. "Maybe we're not the only ones he screwed over."

Cody cut him a glance. "So you're here for someone else."

Brent swept a glance at the room. "Bull riding not paying as well as it used to?"

"It pays just fine. This is the best room in the motel."

Another sweep of his pale green gaze and Brent grinned. "That's not saying much."

"Yeah, well a room's a room." Cody's gaze collided with Brent's and held steady. "You didn't answer my question. Is there somebody else after Sawyer?"

"Maybe."

He studied his brother a moment longer. "You suck at lying," he finally said.

Tense silence wound around them for a long moment before Brent shrugged again. "I had some time off. I saw the magazine. I figured I'd come down and get in a little target practice before my next assignment."

Back in the old days—after The Turning—Brent had become one of the most ruthless hired guns in Texas. Now he called himself a bodyguard and worked for the highest bidder. Some were rich. Some were famous. Some were both. All of them were scared.

"I thought you were in France with Brad and Ang?"

"That was last year. I quit. The money was good, but following around a bunch of kids isn't my style."

Brent was every bit the adrenaline junkie that Cody was and so he thrived on danger. "I've been in Brazil running interference between a high-ranking political official and a local drug cartel that wants him six feet under."

"How the hell did you see an American motorcycle mag in Brazil?"

"Señor Juarez has a thing for Harleys. He's got a huge collection of bikes and he subscribes to all the industry magazines."

"So you saw the article and headed here?"

"I see all those bulls haven't knocked anything loose yet."

"What about Juarez? Doesn't he still have a target on his back?"

"He'll find someone else to keep the wolves at bay. No big deal."

Because nothing was a big deal to Brent since the night Garret Sawyer had robbed them of everything—their family, their humanity. While he couldn't avoid The Turning once a year, he didn't hang around and exchange words the way Colton and Travis did. He was too busy rushing off to the next job, raking in the cash, refusing to look back. To feel the pain. The remorse.

He didn't seem to have a problem with revenge, however.

"Where is he?" Brent's voice was easy and casual, as if he'd asked the time of day. But Cody didn't miss the hard glint in his eyes and the stern set of his jaw.

"Out of town. He gets back on Friday."

"That sucks."

Boy, did it ever.

Not only did Cody have to wait around for the next three days, but he had to stay away from Miranda.

He *would* stay away from her.

Especially now.

Now that he loved her.

He really and truly *loved* her.

The knowledge sat heavy inside of him and made him all the more determined. No way was Cody going to break her heart the way his bastard of a father had broken his mother's. He couldn't guarantee a future and so he was getting the hell out of Dodge just as soon as he ended Sawyer's miserable existence.

If he ended it.

He pushed aside the doubt. Of course he was killing Sawyer. The vampire had taken everything from Cody and his brothers. *Everything*.

Once Friday hit, Garret Sawyer would be history.

Until then, Cody was keeping his damned head on straight and remembering who he was. What he was.

He eyed his older brother. "So are you going to stick around and help me?"

Brent grinned, but the expression didn't quite reach his eyes. "I didn't travel thousands of miles to let you have all the fun."

SHE WAS *NOT* FALLING FOR HIM.

That's what Miranda told herself as she tossed and turned the rest of the night, trying to forget Cody Braddock and the fact that he'd walked away from her.

Even now, tucked safely in her bed, wearing her favorite nightshirt, she wanted to go after him. She wanted it so much that it scared her because she'd never wanted a man the way she wanted Cody Braddock.

A vampire, she reminded herself. Not a man.

He was something unnatural. Larger than life.

It only made sense that she would want him.

But she didn't *need* him. That was the only bright

spot in everything. She wasn't her mother and she wasn't going to end up broken. Her mother hadn't been able to tell the difference between love and lust, but Miranda could. The attraction she felt had everything to do with their physical connection and nothing to do with the fact that she connected with him on a deeper level. That she shared the pain he felt for his own mother because she knew what it was like to lose someone.

She turned onto her side and tried to ignore the past that rushed at her. Memories of a young girl holding her mother's hand, begging her to stay alive because as negligent and weak as her mother had been, Miranda had loved her anyway.

But her mother hadn't loved Miranda back. Not enough to hold on until the ambulance had arrived.

She'd died right there on the living room floor and Miranda had made up her mind to never, *ever* fall for a man so deeply, so intensely that she lost herself. She would never love a man more than everyone else in her life. More than herself.

Not that she had to worry about that at this moment. She didn't love Cody Braddock. She *wouldn't* love him. Even more, she wasn't making the same dumb mistake twice. She might have surrendered tonight, but it wasn't happening again.

The deal was over.

No more list. No more sex.

No more Cody.

Miranda gave up trying to fall asleep, climbed out of bed and headed for the bathroom. Peeling off her clothes, she stepped into a warm shower and let the spray hit her directly in the face.

And then she didn't have to worry about the tears slipping down her cheeks or wonder why in the world she was crying over a man she didn't love.

21

THE NEXT FEW DAYS TURNED OUT to be the worst of Miranda's life.

She overslept on Tuesday and missed Coffee and Comics with the seniors. She locked her keys in the rental car Darrell had given her since her own car still wasn't fixed. She broke her heel during the short walk home. She ripped a hole in her favorite nightshirt crawling into bed that night and stabbed herself in the eye the next morning with the mascara wand.

The bad luck continued throughout the day—she stepped in a pile of dog poop on the way to work, accidentally deleted part of next week's schedule on her computer, then set Mr. Periwinkle's toupee on fire when she was lighting table candles in the senior dining room that evening.

While she made it to work on Thursday morning in time for Muffin Mania—a truth or dare type game followed by muffins and juice on the patio—she still missed most of the fun due to a mix-up in the food delivery for Friday night's sock hop. Once she'd managed to get two hundred spicy mini burritos (a definite no-no with her clientele) exchanged for the requested pigs-in-a-blanket, it was already well past noon.

She ended up eating leftovers for lunch in the dining room—chipped beef and Jell-O—because she'd forgotten to bring her own.

"You've definitely got something on your mind," Martha told her when they both hit the cafeteria at the same time. The old woman had missed the meal, too, thanks to an addiction to the much-loved *Times of Our Lives,* a new soap opera that aired at noon. "A man?" she asked when Miranda mistook a glass of prune juice for iced tea.

"Not exactly."

"Either *he* is or *she* isn't." The old woman took a bite of her own Jell-O. "In any case, I'm here if you need me. And just so's you know, I've got oodles of experience when it comes to matters of the heart. Been counseling my granddaughter for ages."

"The accountant?"

"That's the one."

A grin tugged at Miranda's lips. "The single accountant?"

"It ain't my fault if she don't listen to what I tell her. She's too interested in them stuffy types and they're more interested in work. There's never any sparks. You gotta have the sparks. Preferably a great big Roman candle, but one of those itty bitty sparklers will work, too. Just so long as it's enough fireworks to put a gleam in your eye. Like the one you got in yours. You're a lucky gal. Very lucky."

Miranda's head snapped up and for a split second, she would have sworn that Martha was taking about Cody Braddock. "Excuse me?"

"That you found Mr. Starch Pants. You've obviously got a nice little fireworks show going on between the two of you judging by the look on your face."

"Um, yeah." Sort of. Greg was lacking in the romance department and he wasn't the most thoughtful man, but he was the right man.

The only man, she told herself for the millionth time since Cody had walked into her life.

Martha eyed her and she had the unnerving feeling that the woman was seeing a lot more than she wanted her to. "You do love him, don't you?"

Yes was right there, but it stalled on the tip of her tongue. "There are more important things than love."

"Really? Like what?"

"Trust. Respect."

"I trust Morty Milner over there," she pointed an arthritic finger at a small, frail man with eyeglasses and a *lot* of nose hair. "The man was a judge for years and he's the fairest person I know. I also respect him, but you couldn't get me down the aisle with him if you had a cattle prod poking me in the ass." She wagged her Jell-O spoon. "Love is *the* most important thing and if anybody tells you different, they've never been in love. I was married to my dear Arnold for forty-five years and they were the best of my life."

"But what if it's a bad love?" Miranda finally asked after a long, silent moment. "One that brings out the worst in you?"

"Love is love, sugar. It brings out the worst in all of us, and the best. That's the beauty of it."

But there was nothing beautiful about what had

happened to Miranda's mother. She'd died a broken woman. And all because she'd fallen in love.

Not this girl.

Miranda held tight to her resolve, but it did little to calm the anxiety that ate away inside of her as the day wore on.

It was *Thursday*.

Cody would face off with the vampire who'd killed his family tomorrow night and then he would leave Skull Creek for good.

If he survived.

Either way, she would never see him again.

Never touch him. Never talk to him.

The notion should have been comforting. Instead, it ate away at her as she headed home and spent another restless night trying to forget the one man who'd turned her world upside down.

No matter how sure Martha had been of her words, she'd obviously never experienced the bad side of love. She'd never seen the devastation, never felt the pain.

But Miranda had seen and felt both. It was a lesson she'd learned early on. One she would never forget.

No matter how much she suddenly wanted to.

CODY MEANT TO STAY AWAY from her. He really did.

He managed to do just that, too, but when he opened his eyes Friday evening, he could no longer resist. He wasn't sure what he was going to say, he just knew that staying away was killing him.

His gaze skittered to the window and the faint glow of dusk that outlined the shades before shifting to the vampire stretched out on the chair. Brent was still sound asleep, his entire body deathly still, his cowboy hat tipped low over his forehead, hiding his face.

Awareness zipped up and down Cody's spine and anxiety pulsed through him. His gut clenched and he knew it was time.

Garret was back.

He took a quick shower and dressed in a T-shirt and jeans. He was just pulling on his boots when he heard his brother's voice.

"Keep it down, would ya?" Brent still had the hat tipped low, his body still sprawled in the chair.

"I've got to go out for a little while. I'll swing by in an hour to pick you up."

"I'll be ready. Now get out before I kick you out. I need my beauty sleep."

"Nice to see that you're still as bossy as ever."

"That's what big brothers are for."

Cody grinned, the expression fading as he pulled open the door and stepped out onto the front walk. He cast a quick glance around and tuned his senses for any sign of Benny James. The man had been invisible for the past few days, but Cody had known he was there anyway. He'd been asking questions around town. The diner. The local convenience store. While Cody had managed to keep to himself and hole up in his room most of the time, he knew that someone, somewhere had seen him. And that someone would tell Benny. And the man would stick around even longer.

Cody listened for the frantic beat of a heart, the sharp intake of breath.

Nothing.

He heard only the sound of the ice machine and the clatter of binoculars as Eldin lowered his Nikon's and shot Cody a quick salute from the lobby window.

He acknowledged the man and headed for his truck. Climbing behind the wheel, he gunned the engine and pulled out of the drive. Hanging a left toward the senior center, he ignored the warning that went off in his head and told him he was about to make the biggest mistake of his life.

Just leave, already.

But he couldn't.

He wasn't sure what he was going to say to her. He just knew he had to see her one more time.

One last time.

"IF EULA KEEPS TWISTING like that, she's liable to throw out her hip." Beula stuffed a pigs-in-the-blanket into her mouth and eyed her sister who stood in the middle of the dance floor wearing a pink poodle skirt and cat's eye glasses. "That or she's liable to give herself a hernia."

"I'd prefer the hernia to the hip," Mildred Stockton said. She sipped her pink milkshake (made with lactose-free milk) and eyed the dance floor. "I wish I could do that."

"You should try," Miranda told her. "It's easy."

"You won't get me out there," Beula huffed. "Not with my arthritis."

"Come on, Miss Mildred." Miranda took the old woman's hand. "I'll dance with you."

"Careful, Mildred," Dora Lee's voice followed them. "She'll have you pole-dancing before the night's over."

"Why don't you tell that old biddy where to go?" Mildred asked when they reached the dance floor. "You shouldn't let her be so mean to you."

"It doesn't matter what she says." It didn't, Miranda realized as she started to twist. She could feel Dora Lee's eyes on her, yet the disapproval she saw didn't bother her as much as it usually did.

Nothing could make her feel as awful as she'd felt the past few days without Cody Braddock.

As if her thoughts had conjured him, she saw him filling up the doorway. He looked as handsome as ever in a black T-shirt and faded jeans. His hair was disheveled, as if he'd run his hands through it too many times to count. His mouth was pulled into a tight line. His eyes sparkled, so hot and molten and her breath caught.

"I need to go and check on the refreshments," she told Mildred before leaving the old woman dancing with the others. She headed for the opposite side of the room, determined to keep as much distance between her and Cody as possible.

Distance was good. Distance would save her.

The twist faded into a slow, soulful song that hollowed out her stomach and made her swallow.

"Can I have this dance?" Cody's deep voice slid into her ears. Her mouth dried out and her nipples pebbled and every nerve in her body throbbed to full awareness. She knew then that running away wasn't going to solve her problem. It was here, standing behind her, waiting.

She drew in a deep, shaky breath and sent up a silent prayer for strength.

And then she turned around.

22

"I DON'T THINK THAT'S A GOOD idea," Miranda said the moment her gaze collided with his.

"Why not?"

"Because I'm not exactly at my sanest when I'm close to you."

"Because I'm a vampire?"

Because I'm weak. Because I want you. Because I can't have you.

The reasons rushed through her head before she could stop them, but she didn't say them out loud.

It didn't matter. He knew. He stared at her, into her, and he felt every one. And damned if it didn't bring the faintest smile to his face.

Her heart clenched and she barely resisted the urge to press her lips to the small dimple that cut into his jaw. She opened her mouth to say *"This isn't funny,"* but Dora Lee's voice cut her off.

"I knew it was just a matter of time before all the undesirables followed her here." The woman stood at the punch bowl, talking to one of the new residents, a short, round woman by the name of Ruby Honeycutt. Ruby was eighty years old and she thrived on a juicy piece of news. Her eyes practically bugged out of her head as she stared at Cody.

"Oh, my."

"Next thing you know," Dora Lee went on, "she'll be setting up shop in her office and this place will be no better than one of them brothels. Why, I wouldn't be surprised if we get raided by the police."

"Oh, *my*."

The talk reminded her of many similar scenes from her past. There'd been so much gossip. So many derogatory comments. So many lies. And not once had Miranda ever stood up for herself.

She'd understood why people had talked and so she'd let them.

She summoned her courage and turned toward Dora Lee. "He's not an undesirable. He's my guest. Not that it's any of your business. What I do, who I do it with— it's none of your business." And then she took Cody's hand and led him toward the dance floor.

"I'm impressed."

"Because I can be a bitch?"

"Because you can do it so well."

"I don't know if I should be flattered or offended."

"Just say thanks."

"Thanks."

Before she could rethink her rash decision to dance with him, he drew her close. His arms surrounded her and his scent filled her nostrils and the urge to lean against him was nearly unbearable.

One dance, she told herself. Then she would make

up an excuse and retreat to her office. He would leave. And that would be the end of it.

The end.

"Just breathe." His deep voice distracted her from her thoughts a split second before he killed the last inch of distance between them and pulled her flush against his body.

"Easy for you to say. You don't have to bother with it."

He chuckled softly and tightened his grip on her waist.

The music pulsed around them as Otis Redding crooned about *these arms* and *holding tight* and for the next few moments, Miranda forgot everything except the feel of Cody's body against hers. It had only been a few days, but she'd missed him so much that it hurt.

"I missed you, too."

Her head snapped up and her gaze collided with his. "I hate when you do that."

"Do what?"

"Read my mind."

"It's actually a little crazy. I can usually only do it when I'm staring into someone's eyes, but you're different. I can *feel* what you're thinking."

Likewise.

There was no mistaking the desperation that pulsed through him. The desire. The need. He'd missed her as well, and try as he might, he'd yet to figure out how he was going to let her go.

Before she could stop herself, she rested her head on his shoulder, closed her eyes and gave herself up to the happiness of being in his arms.

They moved to and fro for a few long moments before his deep voice slid into her ear.

"I waited for you at the gazebo on Tuesday night."

"You did not."

"I wanted to."

The sincerity in his voice made her heart beat that much faster. "I was really busy."

"Haven't you figured out by now that you can't lie to me?"

She couldn't, but she could still lie to herself, which was exactly what she was trying to do. This wasn't about what other people thought about her. It was about what she thought about herself. What she knew deep down inside. What she feared.

"Stop it," she blurted, pulling away from him before the song ended. She started for her office, but barely made it two steps before he caught her arm and hauled her around to face him.

"What?" she blurted. "What do you want from me?"

He looked undecided for a split second as if he wanted to tell her about the emotion pushing and pulling inside of him, but then his expression closed.

His lip met hers and his tongue plunged deep and, just like that, he was kissing her. The assault was fast and furious and desperate, and she couldn't help herself.

She kissed him back.

She slid her arms around his neck and gave herself up to the feel of him. He tasted even better than she remembered. Sweeter. More intoxicating. Her breath stalled and her body trembled and desire rushed through her as furious as a raging river and just as deadly.

And then it was over.

He looked as shocked as she felt as he stared down at her.

By her reaction.

By his own.

"I don't want anything from you." *I want everything.* That's what his gaze said. But his lips refused to voice it. Instead, he murmured, "I just wanted to say goodbye."

She fought the urge to throw herself into his arms and beg him not to go.

But years of fighting her own nature, of bottling it up and burying it deep, welled up inside her and she held back.

"Goodbye."

He eyed her a long moment, and then he turned and started to walk away.

She let him.

Blinking frantically, she fought back the tears that welled in her eyes and tried to ignore the thought that she'd just given up the one thing that mattered most.

She still had it. Her pride. Her heart.

"I told you," Dora Lee's voice jerked her back to reality. "She's no better than her mother and her trashy sisters."

Miranda became painfully aware of the dozens of eyes that turned on her. Mr. Witherspoon and Mr. Jacoby who stood near the punch bowl. Eula and Beula who danced with each other a few feet away. Martha who sat near the DJ table and tapped her feet.

It was one thing to tell off Dora Lee about her rude comments and quite another to make a fool of herself in front of everyone.

"I need to check on the punch," she blurted, beating a hasty retreat toward her office.

She shut the door and sank down into her chair, her hands trembling, her stomach doing somersaults.

She'd kissed him. In front of God and everyone. She'd forgotten the past, the present, the future, and she'd *kissed* him.

So?

It wasn't like she'd ripped off her clothes and had sex with him. It was just a kiss. Innocent compared to the things they'd done in the past few days.

But there'd been nothing innocent about her reaction. Her pounding heart. Her trembling thighs. Her quivering breasts. She hadn't ripped off her clothes, but she'd wanted to.

She'd wanted it more than anything.

She was following in her mother's footsteps, all right, falling for a man she couldn't have.

Falling?

She'd already hit the ground. Hard.

She realized that as she stared at the latest e-mail from Greg. Two short lines about how he'd rather have prerecorded classical music for the reception instead of a DJ or a band.

Classical. She hated classical. Even more, they couldn't dance to classical. No soulful Otis blaring from the speakers. No bodies pressed together. No sensual moving against one another. Because Greg wasn't sensual. He was the kind of guy who proposed via e-mail rather than dropping to one knee and pledging his undying love. The kind of guy who just assumed she'd say yes because it made sense. *They* made sense.

He was no-nonsense. Practical. Safe.

The exact opposite of Cody Braddock.

His raw, masculine scent clung to her. His strength pulsed through her. She could feel his anguish as he walked to his truck, his anger as he hauled open the door and climbed behind the wheel. He wanted to walk back in, toss her over his shoulder and haul her back to his motel room.

He wanted one more night with her.

One more moment.

And so did she.

She loved him and suddenly the thought of spending a few more minutes with him was better than letting him walk away right now.

"I just came to say goodbye."

Not yet.

She keyed in the answer she should have given Greg the minute he'd e-mailed her the proposal. *You're great, but you're not the guy for me. I don't like classical and I don't like daisies and I don't want to marry you.*

She hit Send, pushed to her feet and grabbed her purse.

And then for the first time in her life, Miranda let go of her inhibitions and went after what she truly wanted—a cowboy.

Her cowboy.

23

GOODBYE.

Her voice echoed in his head and he drove faster, as if he could outrun the damnable truth.

Though she loved him, she would never admit it.

And what good would it do if she did?

None. Her words wouldn't change anything.

Still, he'd wanted to hear them just once.

He fought the need and hauled ass back to the motel. He would pick up Brent and they would head for Skull Creek Choppers. And then he would get the hell out of this pissant town.

Away from her.

From the damnable feelings eating him up inside.

He slammed on the brakes and swerved into the back parking lot. He was halfway around the side of the motel when he felt the prickling awareness. He came to a dead stop.

For an instant, Cody thought that Benny James might have caught up to him. But then the hair on his arms stood on end and his stomach hollowed out. He knew even before he heard the voice that the moment he'd been waiting for had finally arrived.

"I heard you were looking for me."

He turned and found himself staring at the one face that had haunted him for well over a hundred years.

Garret Sawyer had the same eyes, the same distinct features. The only thing different was that he wasn't covered in blood or holding a knife.

Cody's gaze skittered to either side and he listened for a sound, a thought, *something*. "Where are your friends?"

"This doesn't have anything to do with them. It's between you and me."

"You mean they don't know you're here?" Cody shook his head, remembering Jake McCann's watchdog expression. "That's a little hard to believe."

"This is my fight. I care about them too much to drag them into it."

"And we care about him too much to stay out of it." The vampire Cody had met on his first visit to Skull Creek Choppers stepped from the shadows, along with another vamp, Dillon Cash, the third of the infamous Skull Creek Chopper trio.

"Dammit, Jake," Garret muttered as both vampires came up behind him and flanked him.

"You take him out," Jake added, his gaze riveted on Cody, "We take you out."

Cody shrugged. "It doesn't matter." His attention shifted to Garret, to the face that had been burned into his DNA. Anger and regret whirled inside of him and made his hands clench. His vision fired a bright, vivid red, bathing everything the color of blood. The memories welled up inside of him—his mother's face, the inferno that had been the ranch, the pain of losing it all and being too damned late to do anything—and sent a burst of angry adrenaline pulsing through his body. "All that matters is that you die first." He lunged, slamming into Garret's body.

The vamp fell backward and Cody straddled him.

He slammed his fist into Garret's jaw. Once. Twice. Over and over until he felt the hands reaching for him, pulling him away.

He fought, knowing they would kill him before they let him take out Sawyer, but he didn't care. He should have died that night with his family. He would have if not for Sawyer.

He pushed and pulled, and just like that he was free.

He glanced behind him to see Brent in a hand-to-hand combat with Jake while Dillon Cash picked himself up off the far wall where Brent had flung him. Cody didn't waste a moment. He hit Sawyer running, ramming into him and forcing him backward. He grabbed the vampire's collar and threw him to the pavement. He followed him down and was about to slam his fist into Garret's face again.

"I'm sorry." The words vibrated with pain and something else. Something oddly close to remorse.

Cody didn't buy it for a second, but it startled him anyway. His hand paused, his fist shaking.

Garret's bright red gaze cooled to an icy blue as he stared up at Cody. "I had no choice, man. I had to turn you. You were dying."

"What?"

"I didn't mean to doom you to the hunger, but I didn't know what else to do."

"This isn't about me. It's about my family, you bastard. You killed them and set our ranch on fire."

"You're crazy."

"Are you saying you didn't?"

"The ranch was already blazing when I got there. I didn't kill anyone."

"You were holding the knife. I *saw* you. My oldest brother saw you."

"I used the knife to slit my wrist so that you could drink from me. I found it on the ground."

"You're lying."

"No, he's not." It was Jake's voice. He'd thrown Brent up onto the roof and was picking himself up while Cody's brother scrambled to recover from the hit. "If he says he found it, he found it. And if you have half a brain in that thick head of yours, you'll believe him."

"He's a vampire."

"And a damned good man. He doesn't lie."

"Don't believe him," Brent said as he leapt to the ground. He tossed Cody a very lethal-looking stake that he pulled from the back pocket of his pants. "Kill him."

Cody grasped the deadly piece of wood and held it high, ready to plunge it deep into the vampire's chest.

"Stop!" Miranda's voice rang out. He jerked around in time to see her running toward him. "Please, don't do this. Don't hurt anyone."

"He's a vampire. *The* vampire. And a lying sack of shit. You don't believe him, do you?"

"This isn't about him." She dropped to her knees beside Cody. "This is about you. It doesn't matter what he's done. You're not a killer."

Hearing her voice his greatest fear jabbed at the past and the words came even though he wanted like hell to hold them back. "You're wrong. I killed during the war. And I killed them that night. I wasn't there when I should have been. I let them down and they died because of it."

"They died because some crazy person ended their life. You had nothing to do with that. And if you had been there, you'd be dead, too." Certainty gleamed in her gaze. "You might have made a lot of mistakes in your past, but that wasn't one of them. Bad things happen to good people. It doesn't make any sense sometimes, but we have to deal with that. We can't blame ourselves for other people's mistakes. It wasn't your fault."

As he stared deep into her eyes, he actually believed it. He'd spent so much time searching for peace and he realized then that he wasn't going to find it by killing Garret Sawyer.

No, he'd already found it. With Miranda. She'd saved him with her words, her touch, her love.

She was his peace. His redemption.

And he was hers.

"It wasn't my fault either." Her lips trembled around the words and the tears spilled over. "I spent all this time blaming myself, thinking that if I had been a better kid, she wouldn't have done what she did. But that wasn't it. She died at her own hand. Because of her own weakness."

A car swerved into the parking lot at that moment and car doors slammed. "Garret? Ohmigod!"

Before Cody could blink, a female vampire flew at him, her fangs bared, her eyes a bright, vivid red. She grabbed him by the collar and slammed him up against the motel wall. Brick crumbled and dust flew.

"Stay out of this, Viv." Garret's pained voice drew her attention and she abandoned Cody to fly to his side.

She leaned over him, her touch soft as she cradled his face. "Why didn't you tell us you were coming back early?"

"When Jake mentioned that someone was looking for me, I knew it meant trouble. I wanted you out of it."

"For your information, we're a team. I love you and you love me and that means I'm in it. I can't believe you're so stupid." She slid her arm under his shoulder and helped him to his feet. "You could have gotten yourself staked. We all agreed that we would handle anyone who came after us together. *Together...*"

"That's right." It was the female vampire that Cody had seen with Jake. She reached his side and slid a protective arm around his waist.

"One for all and all for one." The third female marched over to Dillon Cash and let him draw her to his side. "We watch out for each other."

The same way Cody and his brothers had watched out for each other so long ago.

Before they'd lost everything.

While Cody was no longer convinced Garret Sawyer had been responsible, it didn't change the fact that someone had killed his family. Even worse, he might never know the truth.

"Here." Garret's voice drew him from his thoughts and he glanced up to see the vampire looming over him. He held out a hand. "Get up."

Cody hesitated for a moment, but then he let the older vampire pull him up.

"I'm sorry for your loss. I really am. I wish I could give you some answers, but I just don't know. I didn't see anyone there that night. Just you and the other three men. I turned you because you weren't quite dead. That was all I could do."

"You don't remember anything else?"

"Just that it was a busy night."

"What's that supposed to mean?"

"You and your brothers weren't the only ones having a tough time that night. I found three more people a few miles down the road on my way to the next town. Someone had stolen their horses and left them for dead. One of them was already dead, but I managed to save the other two. A man and a woman."

"Who were they?"

"I don't know. He wore a tan vest and a pair of spurs."

"A cowhand?"

"Maybe. I can't remember too much more about him. He looked pretty average. The woman, however, I'll never forget."

"Thanks a lot," Viv said as she came up behind him.

He slid an arm around her waist. "Not because I was attracted to her. She was just different. She had the brightest red hair I'd ever seen and the bluest eyes."

Cody's head snapped up and his gaze traveled the distance to his brother who stood on the side-lines. At Garret's words, Brent looked as if someone had sucker punched him in the gut.

"You don't think it was Rose, do you?" Cody asked.

"We were smack dab in the middle of Apache territory. Did you know anybody else with bright red hair and blue eyes in that area?"

The truth weighed down on Cody as he stood there and faced his brother. Their sister-in-law hadn't died in the fire that night along with everyone else. She was still out there somewhere.

A vampire.

And while Cody still had no clue what had happened that night, he knew deep in his gut that Rose held all the answers.

24

MIRANDA WATCHED CODY leave with his brother. They were headed for Skull Creek Choppers to pick Garret's brain more about what had happened that fateful night.

And while Cody had given her a tender kiss on the lips, it had felt more like a goodbye than a promise of anything to come.

Because he was still leaving.

He feared the demon that lived and breathed inside of him. Not the hunger, but his own nature. He feared that he would hurt her the way his father had hurt his mother. That one day he would grow bored and walk away and she would be devastated.

She feared it, as well, and so she let him go.

But as much as she tried to pretend that it was for the best, she couldn't make herself believe it. She went home and got ready for bed, but she couldn't climb between the sheets and close her eyes.

Instead, she paced her room. Thinking. Wanting.

As scared as she was to love him, she was suddenly more scared not to love him. She wanted to experience what Martha was talking about. She wanted to see the beauty of love just once, and she wanted it with Cody Braddock.

And while it might not last, she was willing to take that chance.

If he felt the same way.

She knew he loved her, but whether or not he was strong enough to act on it, she didn't know. But there was only one way to find out.

Stuffing a suitcase full, she locked up her house and headed for Skull Creek Choppers.

"WE'LL HELP AS MUCH as we can," Garret told him. "Dillon is a computer whiz. If she's out there, he'll track her down and then it's just a matter of doing the legwork."

"And breaking the news to Colton," Brent added.

"We're not telling him anything until we know something for sure," Cody said. "We need to track her down and see for ourselves."

"And what about the woman?" Brent eyed him.

"What woman?"

"That hot little number back at the motel."

"Leave her out of this."

"All I'm saying is that I don't think she'll be too keen on you leaving."

"You think I care?"

Brent arched an eyebrow. "Don't you?"

"What's your point?"

"That I think it's time you stopped trying to avenge us all and let me do a little of the work. I've got my own score to settle."

"I can't do that."

"You can't or you won't?"

"It doesn't matter. I'm going with you regardless." Cody ignored his brother's look and turned back to Garret. He had a few more questions about Rose and then he was getting the hell out of here. The last thing he needed was to slow down. He had Benny James right behind him, a championship year just ahead and Rose out there somewhere. She held all the secrets and he needed to find her.

He would because he sure as hell wasn't staying here and making another huge mistake.

While he'd finally accepted that the past wasn't his fault, it didn't change who he was or the blood that flowed through his veins.

Life father, like son.

It was time to go.

HE WAS A STUBBORN FOOL.

The thought struck as Miranda stared through the glass windows at Cody who stood in the machine shop area of Skull Creek Choppers with his brother, Jake, Garret and Dillon.

He was leaving, all right. She could see it in the stern set of his jaw and the determination that glittered in his gaze. Even more, she felt it deep in her bones.

She summoned her courage, pushed open the door and stepped inside.

Every gaze turned toward her, but she met only one.

"Can I talk to you for a second?"

The room cleared in a heartbeat and they were alone.

"What are you doing here?" Cody finally asked.

"I won't let you walk away from me again."

He shook his head. "I know you think this is what you want, but you deserve better than me. You—"

"I'm going with you." She held up the suitcase. "We'll find her. Then we'll go on the road and you can ride as many bulls as you want. After it's all said and done, we can come back here and settle down. If you love me." She eyed him and insecurity crept into her expression. "You do love me, don't you?"

He loved her, all right. She knew it as she stared deep into his eyes and saw the love gleaming in the rich depths. A comforting warmth vibrated through his body, chased away the cold and coaxed every nerve to full awareness. He felt love, all right.

He felt *alive*.

And afraid.

His body went stiff. Every muscle pulled tight and a grim frown pulled at his mouth. "I appreciate the offer, but I don't think—"

"You're not your father," she cut in. "You're not him anymore than I'm my mother." She closed the distance between them until they stood only an inch apart. "I know that now, but I wouldn't have if I hadn't taken a chance. You showed me how to let go and act on my feelings. That's what you have to do." Her gaze held his. "Slow down long enough to take a chance."

"And if it doesn't work out?" The words were soft, filled with fear and desperation.

Her chest hitched. "You can't live your life being afraid to really *live*." Before he could open his mouth, she added, "That adrenaline rush you get on the back of a bull isn't the same thing. That's eight seconds. This is real." She touched his hand to her heart. "This is life." Her gaze collided with his. "This is *us*. Isn't it worth taking a chance? I never thought so in the past, but I can honestly say now that I'd rather have a few minutes of extraordinary with you than a lifetime of nothing special without you."

"You'd really give up everything for me?"

"*You* are everything. We're connected now."

Linked. Forever and ever.

She sent the silent message and his eyes widened.

"I'm a vampire," he added. "That means no growing old together."

"I know what it means. I'll never have to worry about buying new face creams or a heavy-duty lift bra when things start going south."

"Are you saying what I think you're saying?"

"I love you and I want to spend forever with you. I know exactly what it means."

He pulled her into his arms then and gave her a deep, desperate kiss that told her how much he loved her and cherished her and that she was the best thing that had ever happened to him. And he knew it.

When he finally drew away, she stared up at him. "Does this mean that you're taking me with you?"

"It means that we're going home." A serious expression touched his gaze as he stared down at her. "I didn't come here looking for Garret Sawyer. I came here looking for peace of mind, for a way to ease my own guilty conscience because I hated myself for being such a selfish shit. That's what the bull riding was all about. For those few moments, I didn't have to think about the past. But it was always there when I climbed off. It'll always be there without you."

"What are you saying?"

"That I wanted redemption, and I found it. I found you and I'm never going to let you go. It's high time I retired from bull riding. And while I'll definitely help my brother because I sure as hell want to know the truth, my search is over." He glanced at the vampire who stood in the office, staring at him through the glass. "It's Brent's turn now."

And then he kissed her again.

* * * * *

*Celebrate 60 years of pure reading pleasure
with Harlequin®!*

To commemorate the event, Silhouette Special
Edition invites you to Ashley O'Ballivan's bed-
and-breakfast in the small town of Stone Creek. The
beautiful innkeeper will have her hands full caring
for her old flame Jack McCall. He's on the run and
recovering from a mysterious illness, but that won't
stop him from trying to win Ashley back.

*Enjoy an exclusive glimpse of Linda Lael Miller's
AT HOME IN STONE CREEK
Available in November 2009 from
Silhouette Special Edition®*

The helicopter swung abruptly sideways in a dizzying arch, setting Jack McCall's fever-ravaged brain spinning.

His friend's voice sounded tinny, coming through the earphones. "You belong in a hospital," he said. "Not some backwater bed-and-breakfast."

All Jack really knew about the virus raging through his system was that it wasn't contagious, and there was no known treatment for it besides a lot of rest and quiet. "I don't like hospitals," he responded, hoping he sounded like his normal self. "They're full of sick people."

Vince Griffin chuckled but it was a dry sound, rough at the edges. "What's in Stone Creek, Arizona?" he asked. "Besides a whole lot of nothin'?"

Ashley O'Ballivan was in Stone Creek, and she was a whole lot of somethin', but Jack had neither the strength nor the inclination to explain. After the way he'd ducked out six months before, he didn't expect a welcome, knew he didn't deserve one. But Ashley, being Ashley, would take him in whatever her misgivings.

He had to get to Ashley; he'd be all right.

He closed his eyes, letting the fever swallow him.

There was no telling how much time had passed when he became aware of the chopper blades slowing overhead. Dimly, he saw the private ambulance waiting on the airfield outside of Stone Creek; it seemed that twilight had descended.

Jack sighed with relief. His clothes felt clammy against his flesh. His teeth began to chatter as two figures unloaded a gurney from the back of the ambulance and waited for the blades to stop.

"Great," Vince remarked, unsnapping his seat belt. "Those two look like volunteers, not real EMTs."

The chopper bounced sickeningly on its runners, and Vince, with a shake of his head, pushed open his door and jumped to the ground, head down.

Jack waited, wondering if he'd be able to stand on his own. After fumbling unsuccessfully with the buckle on his seat belt, he decided not.

When it was safe the EMTs approached, following Vince, who opened Jack's door.

His old friend Tanner Quinn stepped around Vince, his grin not quite reaching his eyes.

"You look like hell warmed over," he told Jack cheerfully.

"Since when are you an EMT?" Jack retorted.

Tanner reached in, wedged a shoulder under Jack's right arm and hauled him out of the chopper. His knees immediately buckled, and Vince stepped up, supporting him on the other side.

"In a place like Stone Creek," Tanner replied, "everybody helps out."

They reached the wheeled gurney, and Jack found himself on his back.

Tanner and the second man strapped him down, a process that brought back a few bad memories.

"Is there even a hospital in this place?" Vince asked irritably from somewhere in the night.

"There's a pretty good clinic over in Indian Rock," Tanner answered easily, "and it isn't far to Flagstaff." He paused to help his buddy hoist Jack and the gurney into the back of the ambulance. "You're in good hands, Jack. My wife is the best veterinarian in the state."

Jack laughed raggedly at that.

Vince muttered a curse.

Tanner climbed into the back beside him, perched on some kind of fold-down seat. The other man shut the doors.

"You in any pain?" Tanner said as his partner climbed into the driver's seat and started the engine.

"No." Jack looked up at his oldest and closest friend and wished he'd listened to Vince. Ever since he'd come down with the virus—a week after snatching a five-year-old girl back from her non-custodial parent, a small-time Colombian drug dealer—he hadn't been able to think about anyone or anything but Ashley. When he *could* think, anyway.

Now, in one of the first clearheaded moments he'd experienced since checking himself out of Bethesda the day before, he realized he might be making a major mistake. Not by facing Ashley—he owed her that much and a lot more. No, he could be putting her in danger, putting Tanner and his daughter and his pregnant wife in danger, too.

"I shouldn't have come here," he said, keeping his voice low.

Tanner shook his head, his jaw clamped down hard as though he was irritated by Jack's statement.

"This is where you belong," Tanner insisted. "If you'd had sense enough to know that six months ago, old buddy, when you bailed on Ashley without so much as a fare-thee-well, you wouldn't be in this mess."

Ashley. The name had run through his mind a million times in those six months, but hearing somebody say it out loud was like having a fist close around his insides and squeeze hard.

Jack couldn't speak.

Tanner didn't press for further conversation.

The ambulance bumped over country roads, finally hitting smooth blacktop.

"Here we are," Tanner said. "Ashley's place."

* * * * *

Will Jack be able to patch things up with Ashley,
or will his past put the woman he loves
in harm's way?
Find out in
AT HOME IN STONE CREEK
by Linda Lael Miller
Available November 2009 from
Silhouette Special Edition®

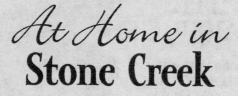

Silhouette Desire

FROM *NEW YORK TIMES* BESTSELLING AUTHOR

DIANA PALMER

THE MAVERICK

A BRAND-NEW LONG, TALL TEXAN STORY

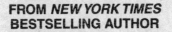

nocturne™

TIME RAIDERS
THE PROTECTOR

by *USA TODAY* **bestselling author**

MERLINE LOVELACE

Former USAF officer Cassandra Jones's unique psychic skills come in handy, as she has been selected to join the elite Time Raiders squad. Her first mission is to travel back to seventh-century China to locate the final piece of a missing bronze medallion. Major Max Brody is assigned to accompany her, and soon Cassandra and Max have to fight their growing attraction to each other while the mission suddenly turns deadly....

Available November
wherever books are sold.

www.silhouettenocturne.com
www.paranormalromanceblog.com

SN61822

The Winter Queen
AMANDA MCCABE

Lady-in-waiting to Queen Elizabeth, Lady Rosamund Ramsay lives at the heart of glittering court life. Charming Dutch merchant Anton Gustavson is a great favorite among the English ladies—but only Rosamund has captured his interest! Anton knows just how to woo Rosamund, and it will be a Christmas season she will never forget....

Available November 2009
wherever books are sold.

REQUEST YOUR FREE BOOKS!

2 FREE NOVELS PLUS 2 FREE GIFTS!

HARLEQUIN®

Blaze™

Red-hot reads!

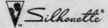

SPECIAL EDITION

FROM *NEW YORK TIMES* BESTSELLING AUTHOR

Ashley O'Ballivan had her heart broken by a man years ago—and now he's mysteriously back. Jack McCall *isn't* the person she thinks he is. For her sake, he must keep his distance, but his feelings for her are powerful. To protect her—from his enemies and himself—he has to leave...vowing to fight his way home to her and Stone Creek forever.

Available in November wherever books are sold.

Visit Silhouette Books at www.eHarlequin.com

COMING NEXT MONTH
Available October 27, 2009

www.eHarlequin.com

HBCNMBPA1009